WRITTEN BY FRANCO

ILLUSTRATED BY SARA RICHARD

LETTERED BY MARSHALL DILLON
EDITED BY JESSE POST
CREATED BY FRANCO AND SARA RICHARD

Bryan Seaton: Publisher/ CEO • **Shawn Gabborin:** Editor In Chief
Jason Martin: Publisher-Danger Zone • **Nicole D'Andria:** Marketing Director/Editor
Danielle Davison: Executive Administrator • **Chad Cicconi:** Who Who
Shawn Pryor: President of Creator Relations

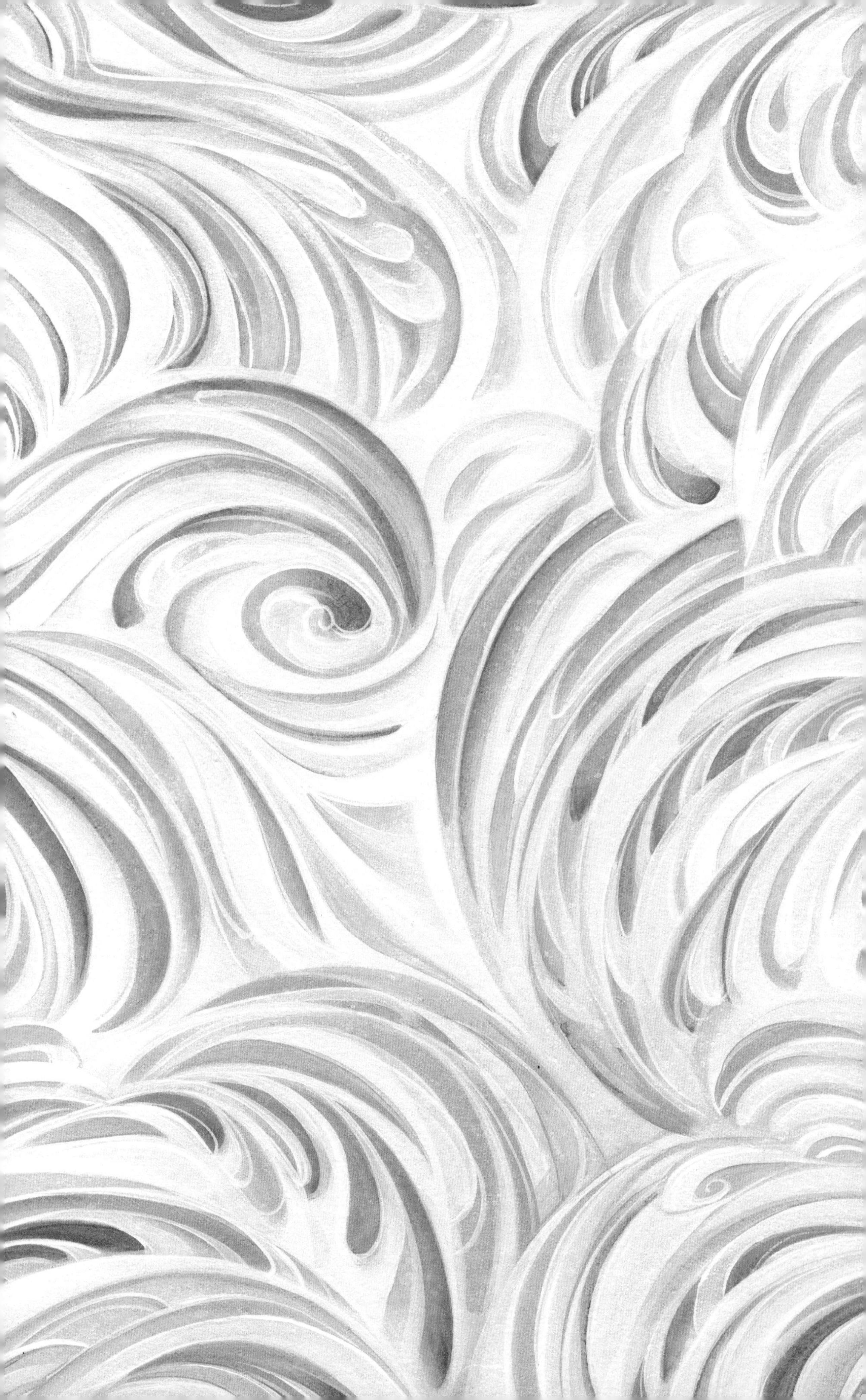

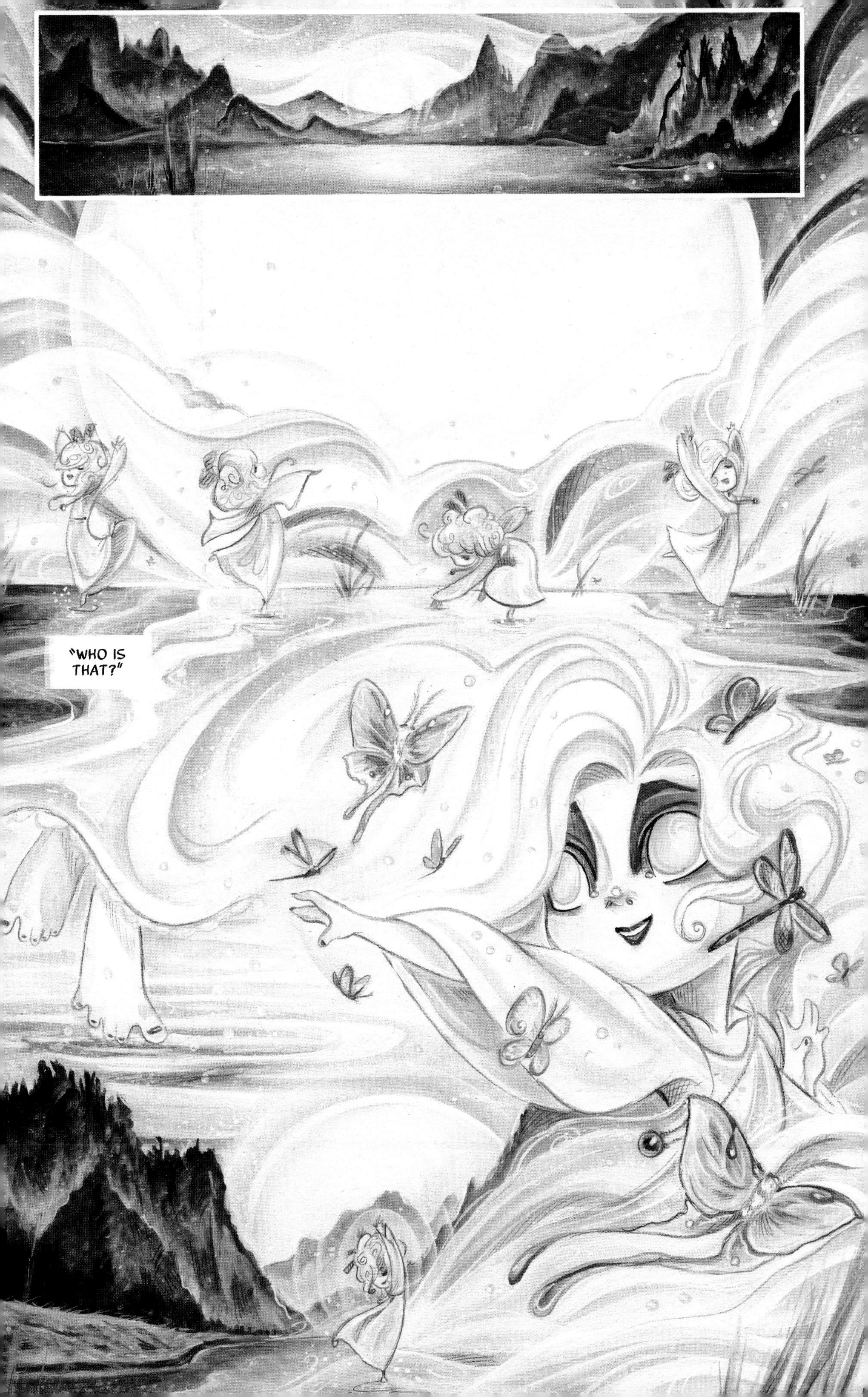
"WHO IS THAT?"

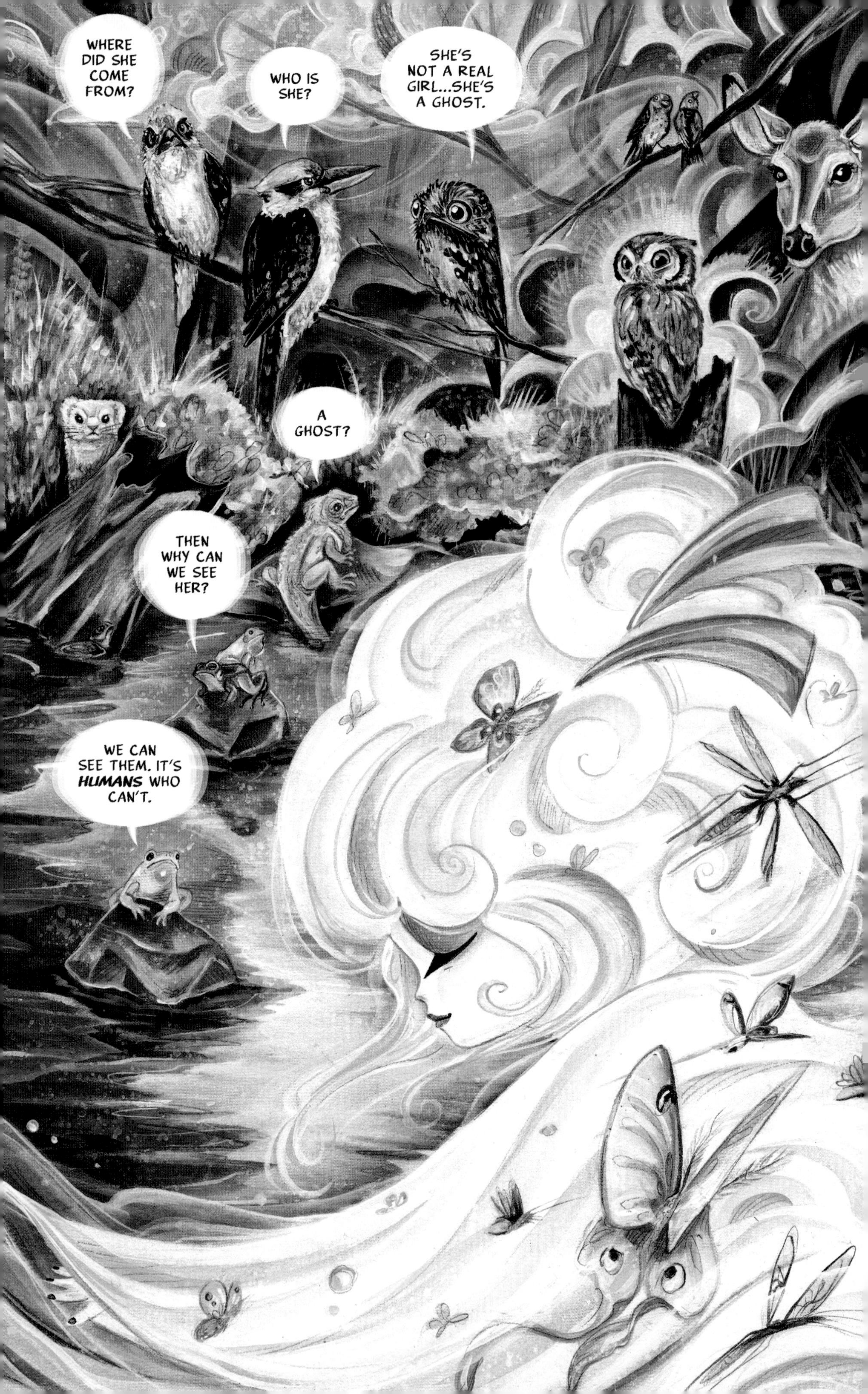
WHERE DID SHE COME FROM?
WHO IS SHE?
SHE'S NOT A REAL GIRL...SHE'S A GHOST.
A GHOST?
THEN WHY CAN WE SEE HER?
WE CAN SEE THEM. IT'S **HUMANS** WHO CAN'T.

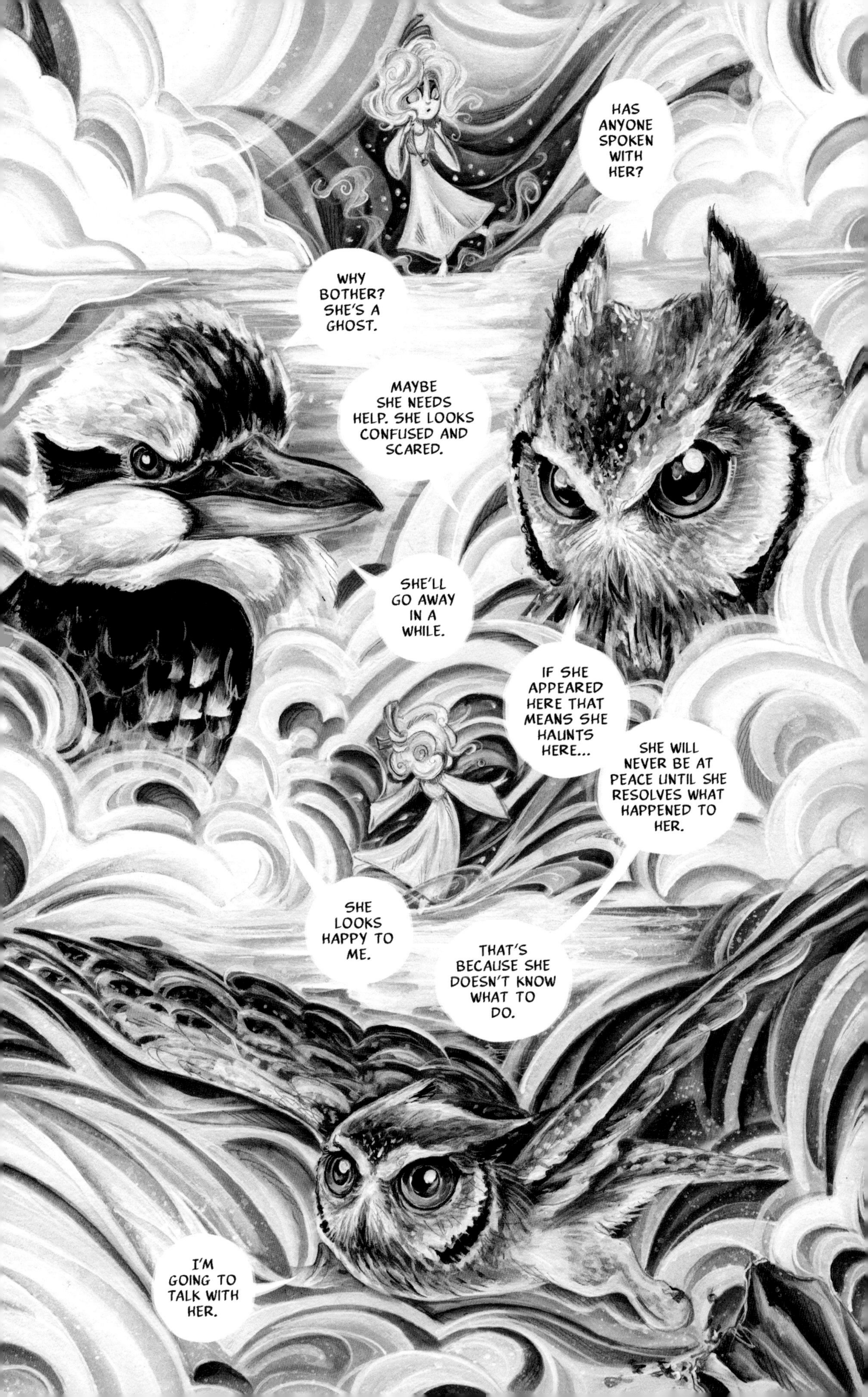
HAS ANYONE SPOKEN WITH HER?
WHY BOTHER? SHE'S A GHOST.
MAYBE SHE NEEDS HELP. SHE LOOKS CONFUSED AND SCARED.
SHE'LL GO AWAY IN A WHILE.
IF SHE APPEARED HERE THAT MEANS SHE HAUNTS HERE...
SHE WILL NEVER BE AT PEACE UNTIL SHE RESOLVES WHAT HAPPENED TO HER.
SHE LOOKS HAPPY TO ME.
THAT'S BECAUSE SHE DOESN'T KNOW WHAT TO DO.
I'M GOING TO TALK WITH HER.

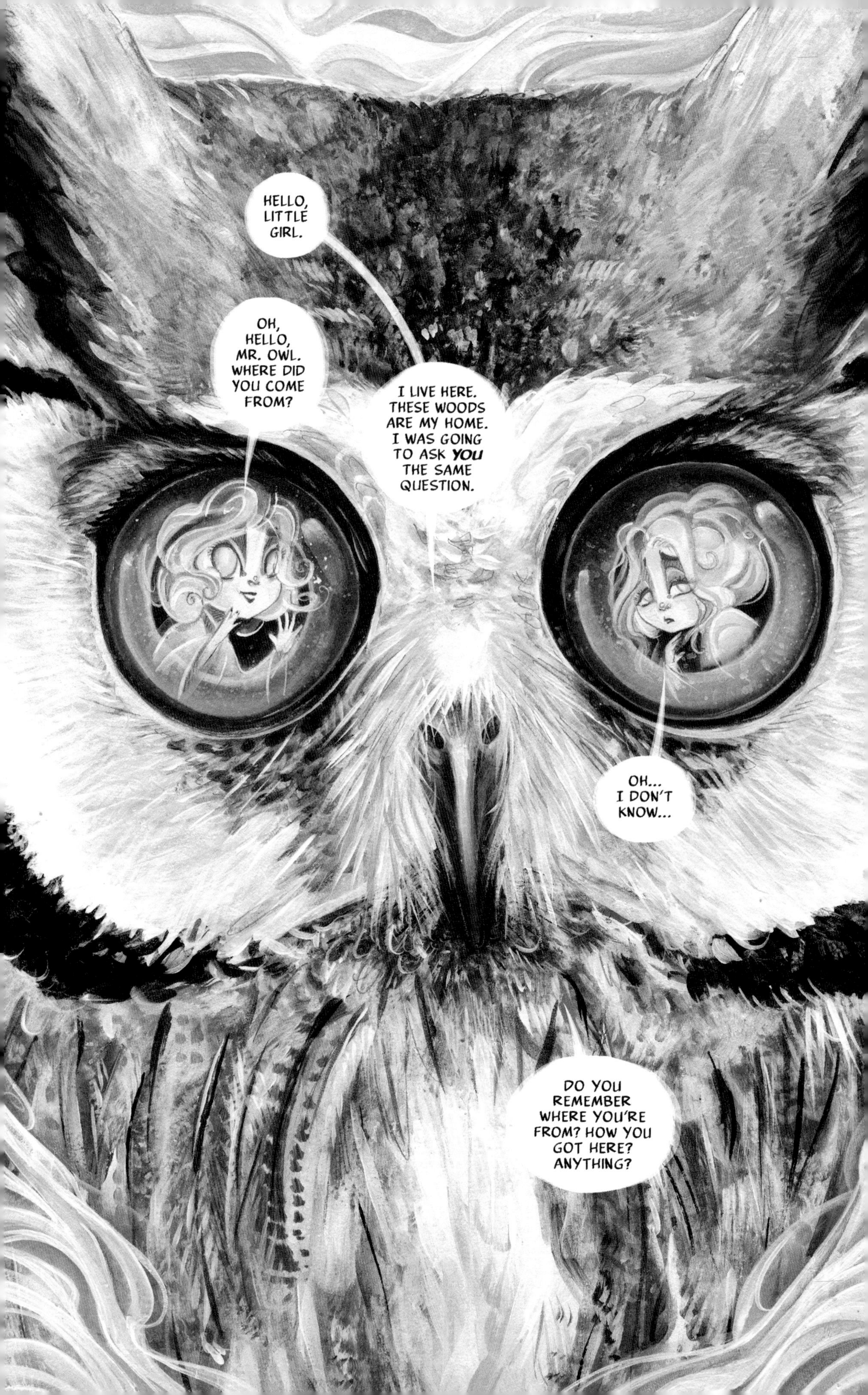
HELLO, LITTLE GIRL.
OH, HELLO, MR. OWL. WHERE DID YOU COME FROM?
I LIVE HERE. THESE WOODS ARE MY HOME. I WAS GOING TO ASK **YOU** THE SAME QUESTION.
OH... I DON'T KNOW...
DO YOU REMEMBER WHERE YOU'RE FROM? HOW YOU GOT HERE? ANYTHING?

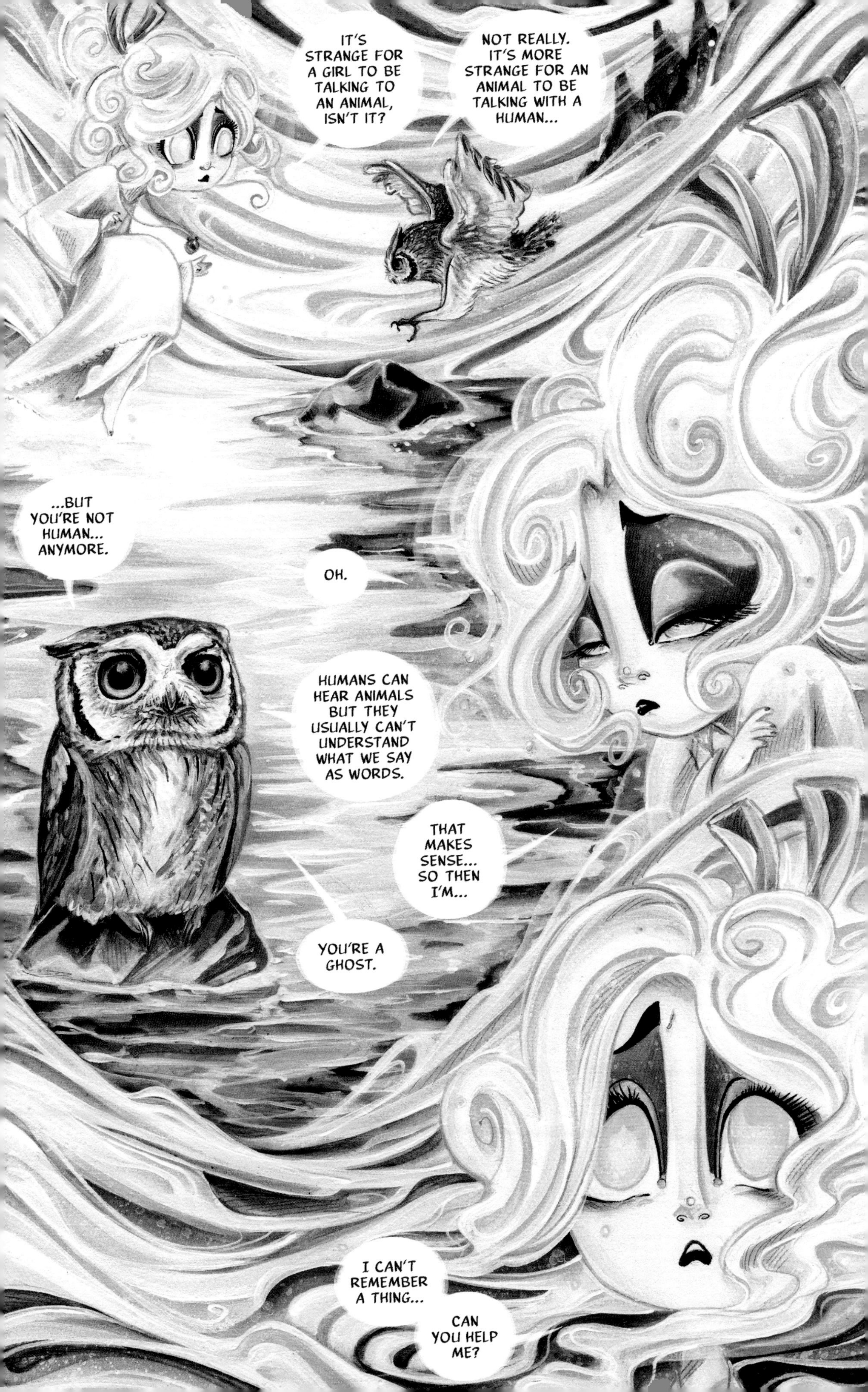
IT'S STRANGE FOR A GIRL TO BE TALKING TO AN ANIMAL, ISN'T IT?
NOT REALLY. IT'S MORE STRANGE FOR AN ANIMAL TO BE TALKING WITH A HUMAN...
...BUT YOU'RE NOT HUMAN... ANYMORE.
OH.
HUMANS CAN HEAR ANIMALS BUT THEY USUALLY CAN'T UNDERSTAND WHAT WE SAY AS WORDS.
THAT MAKES SENSE... SO THEN I'M...
YOU'RE A GHOST.
I CAN'T REMEMBER A THING...
CAN YOU HELP ME?

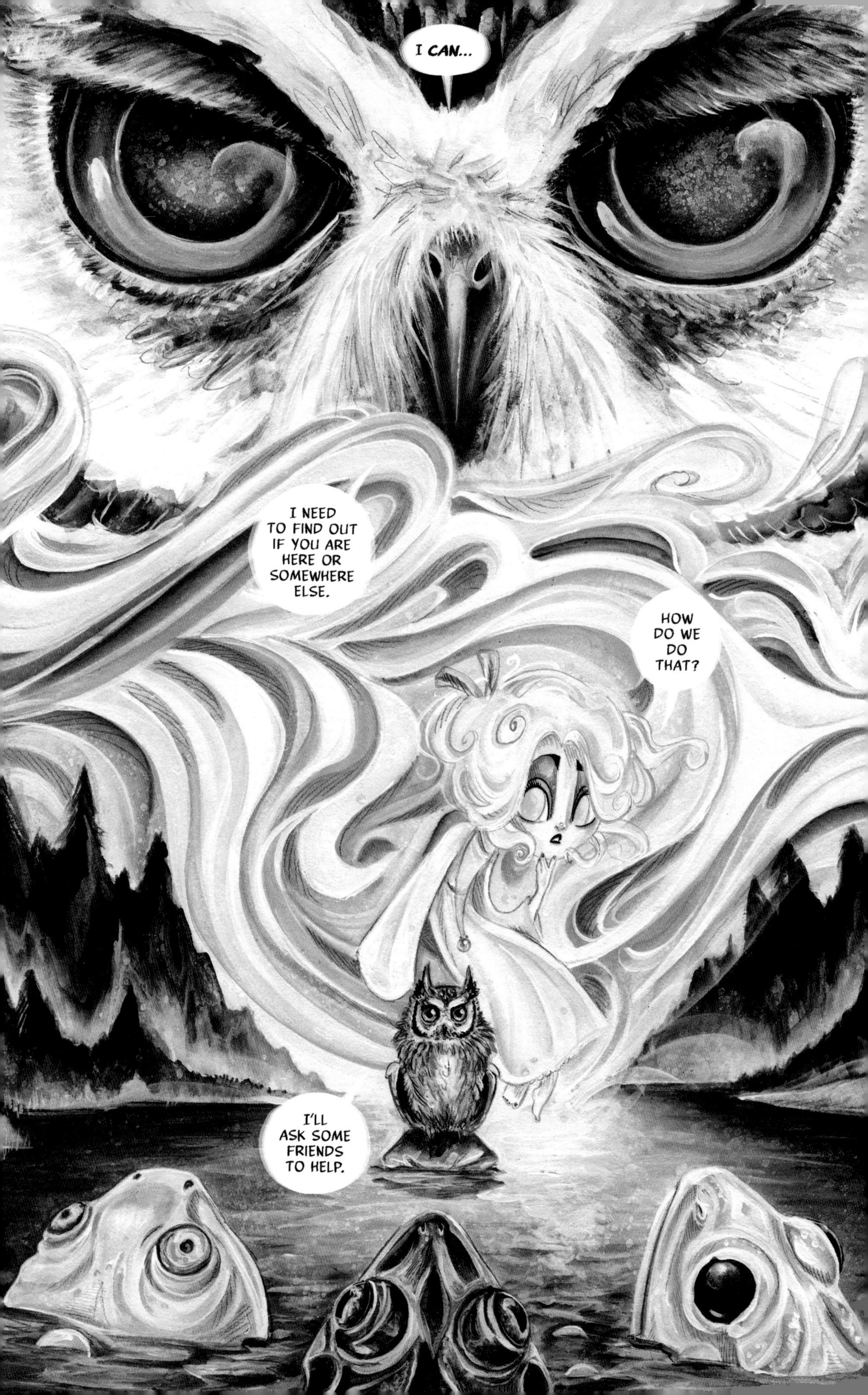
I CAN...
I NEED TO FIND OUT IF YOU ARE HERE OR SOMEWHERE ELSE.
HOW DO WE DO THAT?
I'LL ASK SOME FRIENDS TO HELP.

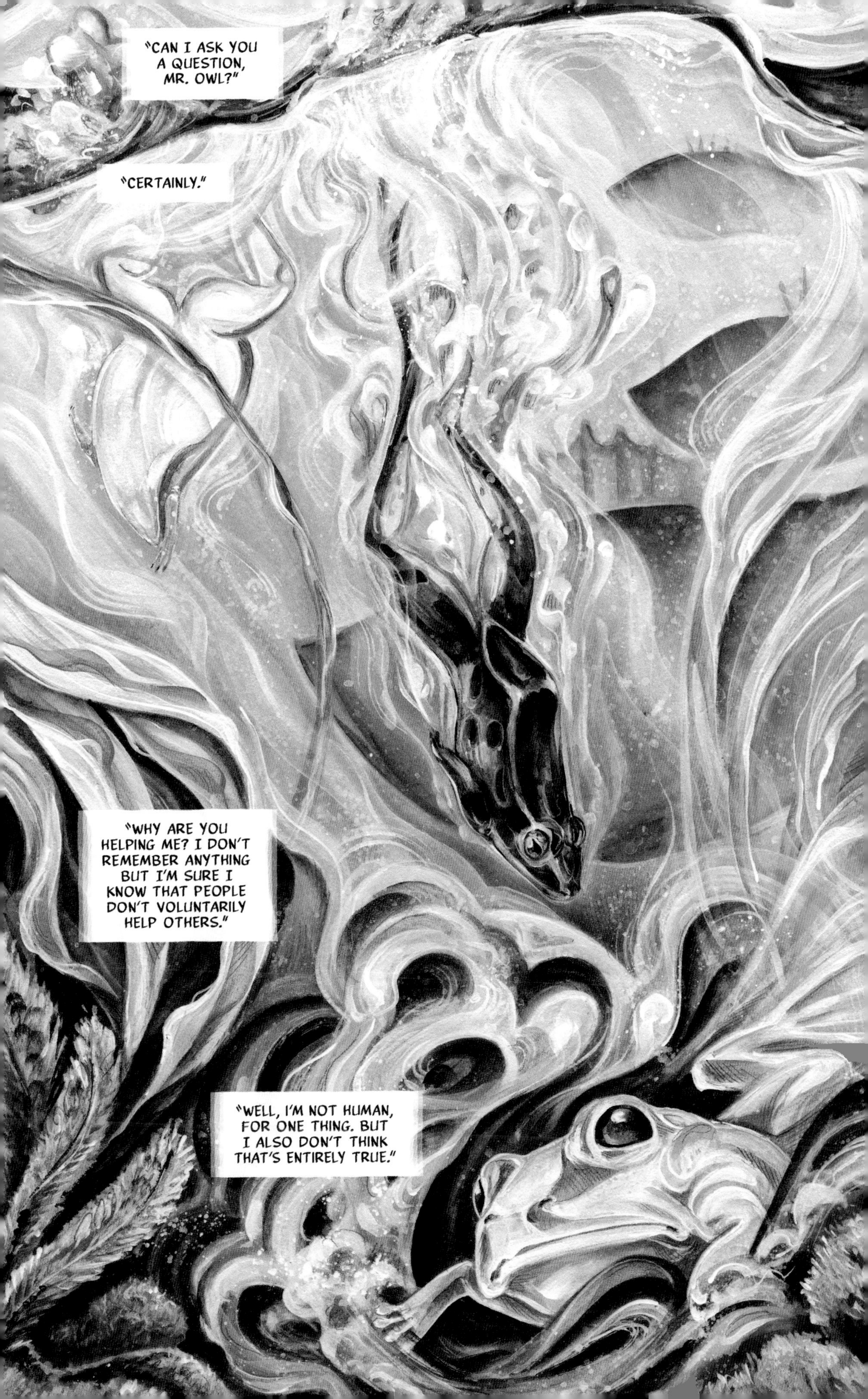
"CAN I ASK YOU A QUESTION, MR. OWL?"
"CERTAINLY."
"WHY ARE YOU HELPING ME? I DON'T REMEMBER ANYTHING BUT I'M SURE I KNOW THAT PEOPLE DON'T VOLUNTARILY HELP OTHERS."
"WELL, I'M NOT HUMAN, FOR ONE THING. BUT I ALSO DON'T THINK THAT'S ENTIRELY TRUE."

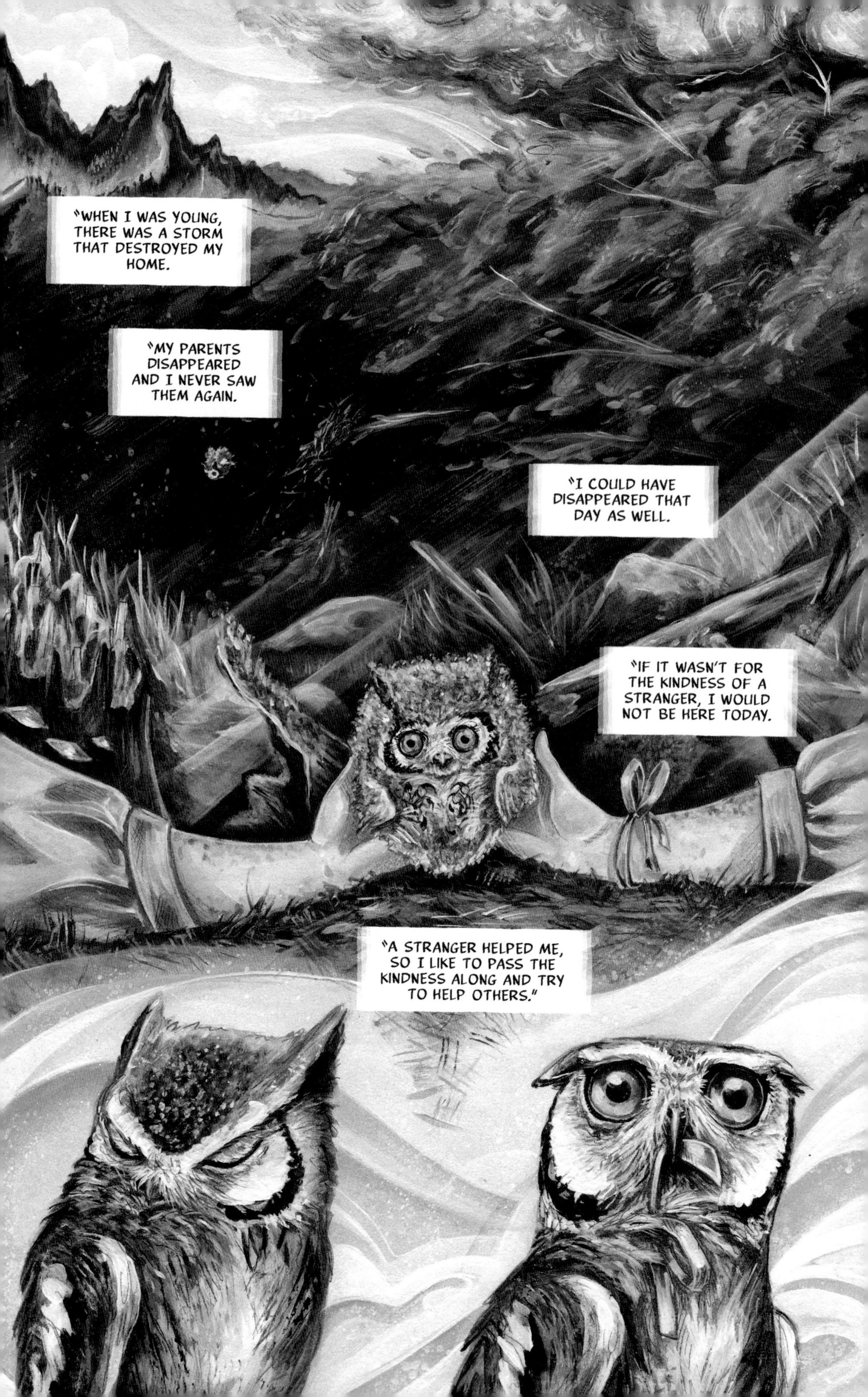
"WHEN I WAS YOUNG, THERE WAS A STORM THAT DESTROYED MY HOME.
"MY PARENTS DISAPPEARED AND I NEVER SAW THEM AGAIN.
"I COULD HAVE DISAPPEARED THAT DAY AS WELL.
"IF IT WASN'T FOR THE KINDNESS OF A STRANGER, I WOULD NOT BE HERE TODAY.
"A STRANGER HELPED ME, SO I LIKE TO PASS THE KINDNESS ALONG AND TRY TO HELP OTHERS."

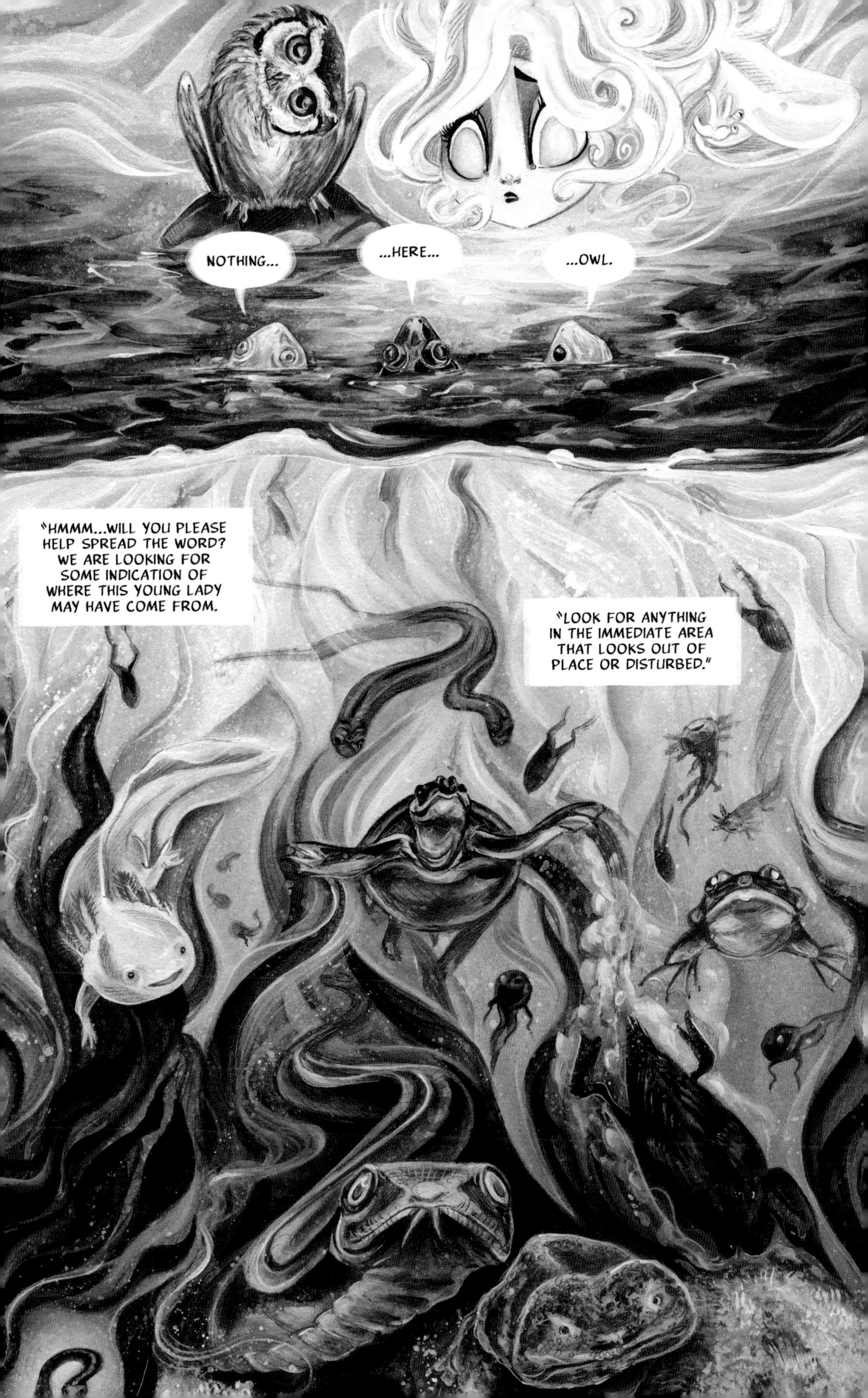
NOTHING...
...HERE...
...OWL.
"HMMM...WILL YOU PLEASE HELP SPREAD THE WORD? WE ARE LOOKING FOR SOME INDICATION OF WHERE THIS YOUNG LADY MAY HAVE COME FROM.
"LOOK FOR ANYTHING IN THE IMMEDIATE AREA THAT LOOKS OUT OF PLACE OR DISTURBED."

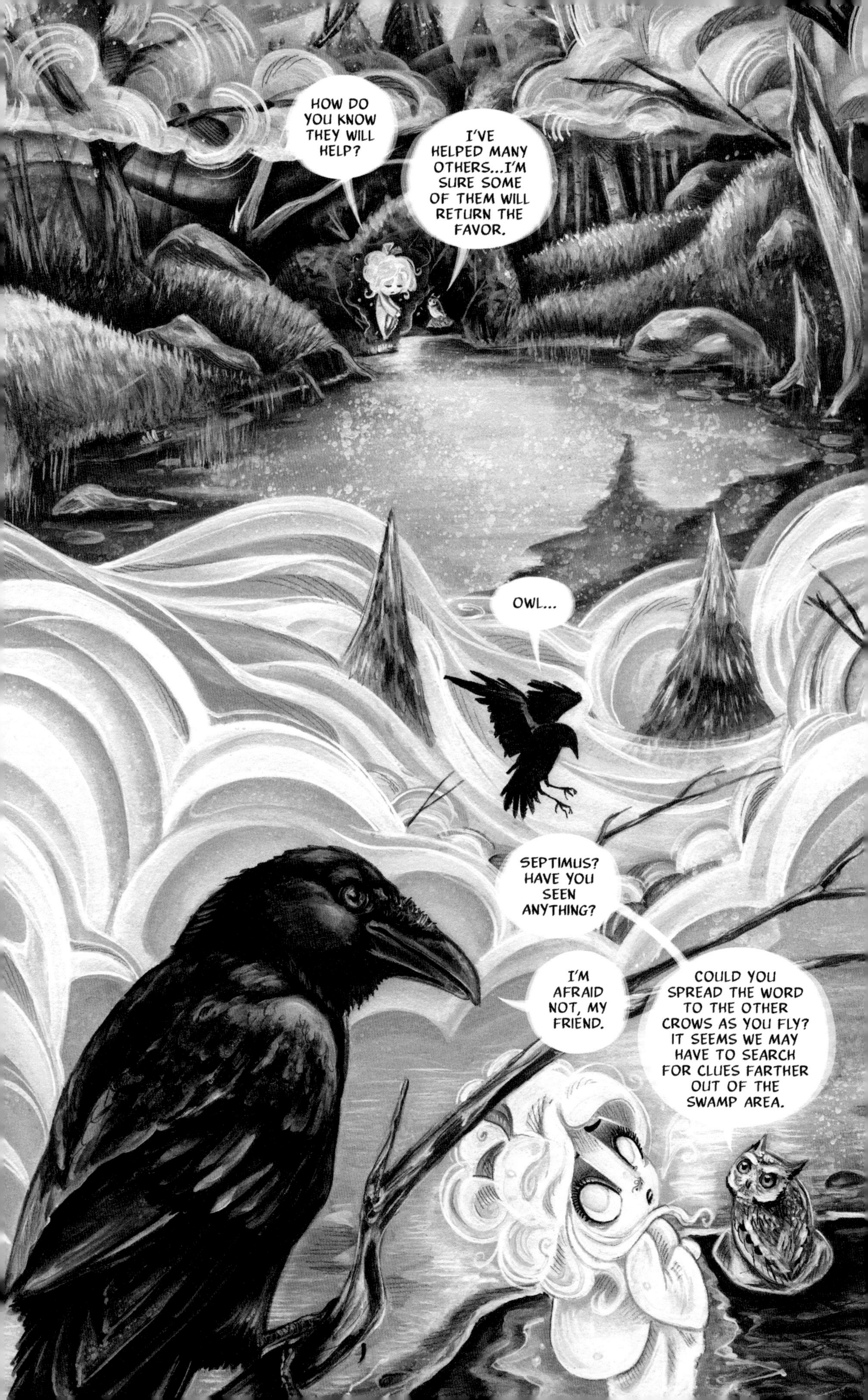
HOW DO YOU KNOW THEY WILL HELP?
I'VE HELPED MANY OTHERS...I'M SURE SOME OF THEM WILL RETURN THE FAVOR.
OWL...
SEPTIMUS? HAVE YOU SEEN ANYTHING?
I'M AFRAID NOT, MY FRIEND.
COULD YOU SPREAD THE WORD TO THE OTHER CROWS AS YOU FLY? IT SEEMS WE MAY HAVE TO SEARCH FOR CLUES FARTHER OUT OF THE SWAMP AREA.

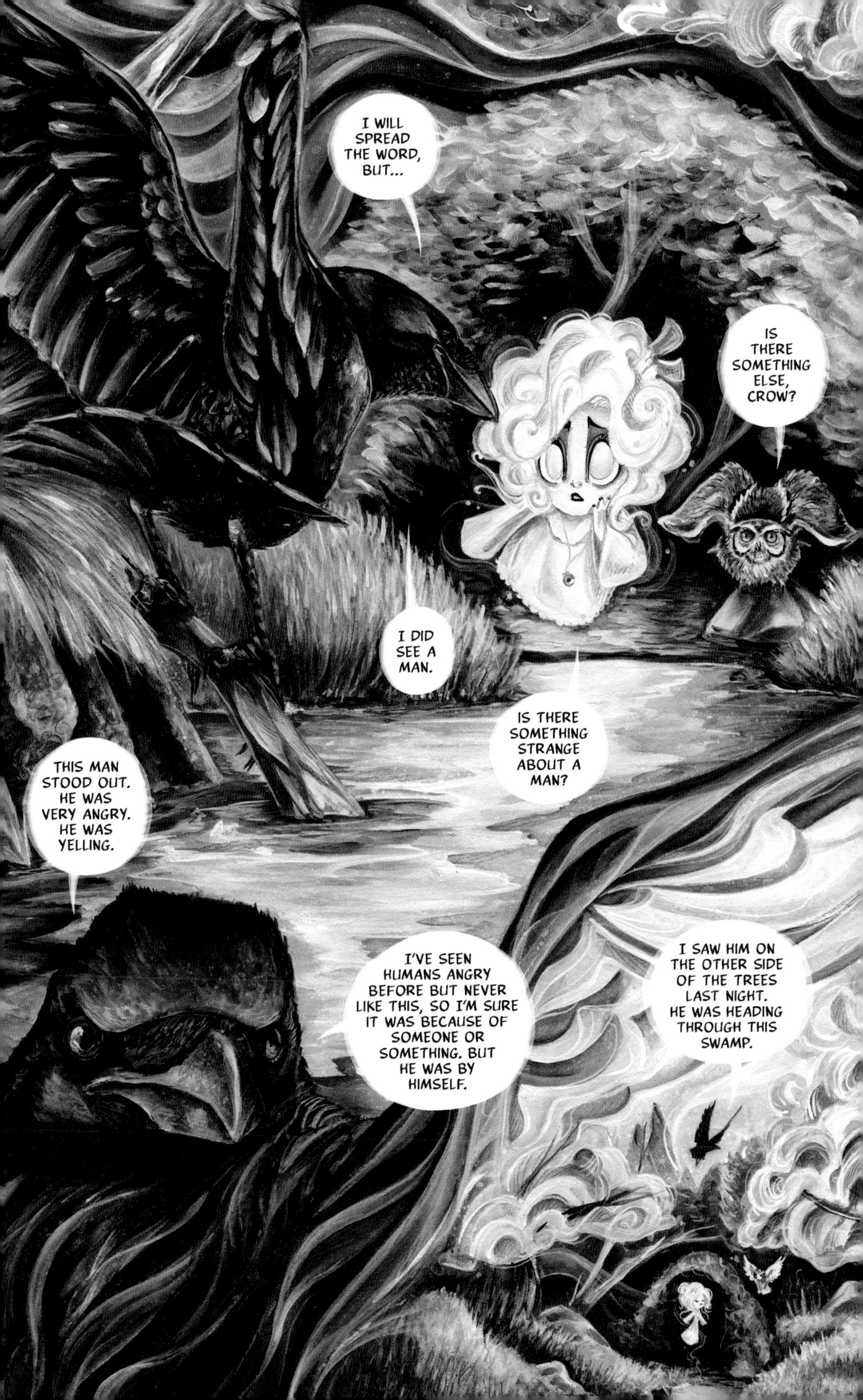
I WILL SPREAD THE WORD, BUT...
IS THERE SOMETHING ELSE, CROW?
I DID SEE A MAN.
IS THERE SOMETHING STRANGE ABOUT A MAN?
THIS MAN STOOD OUT. HE WAS VERY ANGRY. HE WAS YELLING.
I'VE SEEN HUMANS ANGRY BEFORE BUT NEVER LIKE THIS, SO I'M SURE IT WAS BECAUSE OF SOMEONE OR SOMETHING. BUT HE WAS BY HIMSELF.
I SAW HIM ON THE OTHER SIDE OF THE TREES LAST NIGHT. HE WAS HEADING THROUGH THIS SWAMP.

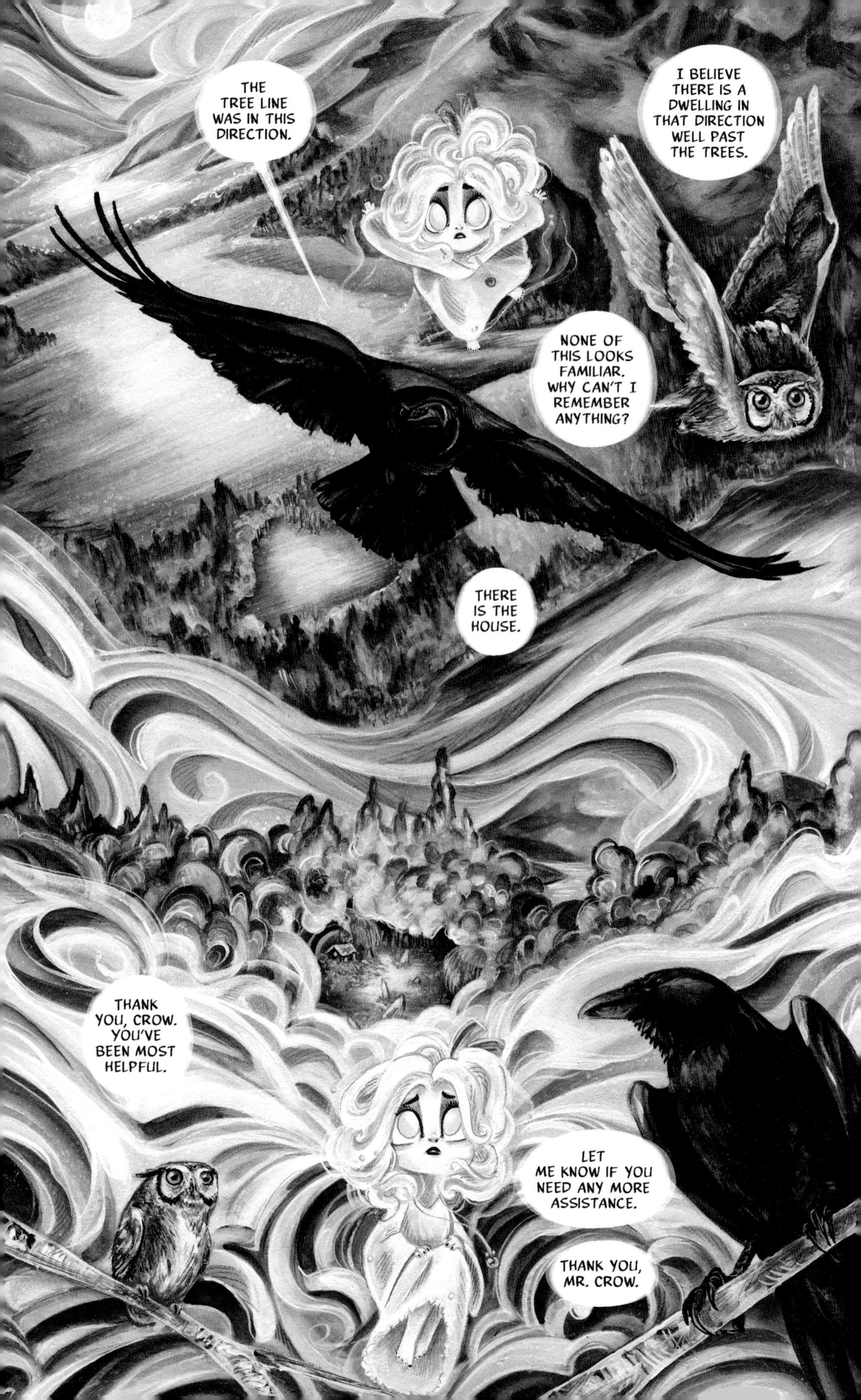
THE TREE LINE WAS IN THIS DIRECTION.
I BELIEVE THERE IS A DWELLING IN THAT DIRECTION WELL PAST THE TREES.
NONE OF THIS LOOKS FAMILIAR. WHY CAN'T I REMEMBER ANYTHING?
THERE IS THE HOUSE.
THANK YOU, CROW. YOU'VE BEEN MOST HELPFUL.
LET ME KNOW IF YOU NEED ANY MORE ASSISTANCE.
THANK YOU, MR. CROW.

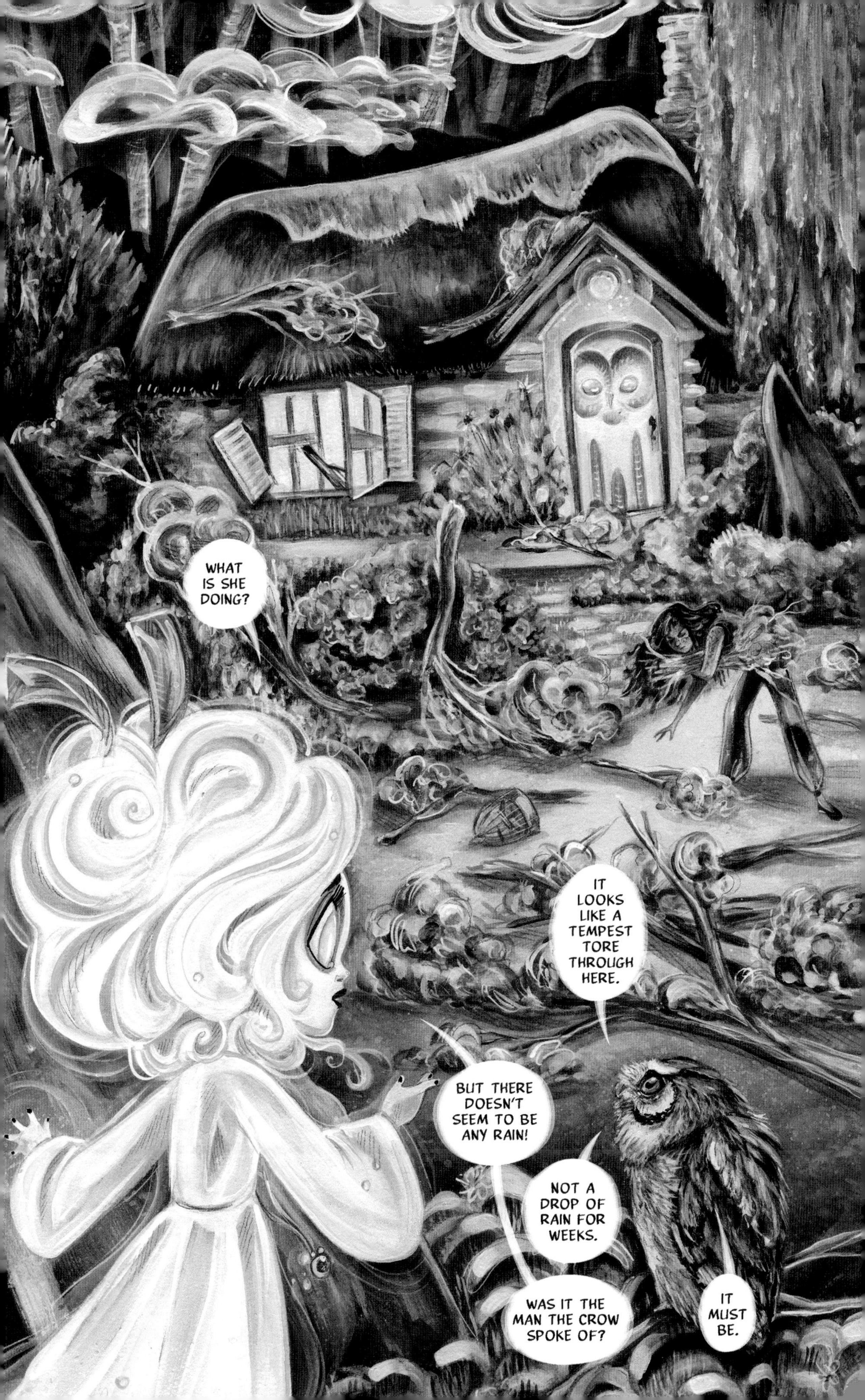
WHAT IS SHE DOING?
IT LOOKS LIKE A TEMPEST TORE THROUGH HERE.
BUT THERE DOESN'T SEEM TO BE ANY RAIN!
NOT A DROP OF RAIN FOR WEEKS.
WAS IT THE MAN THE CROW SPOKE OF?
IT MUST BE.

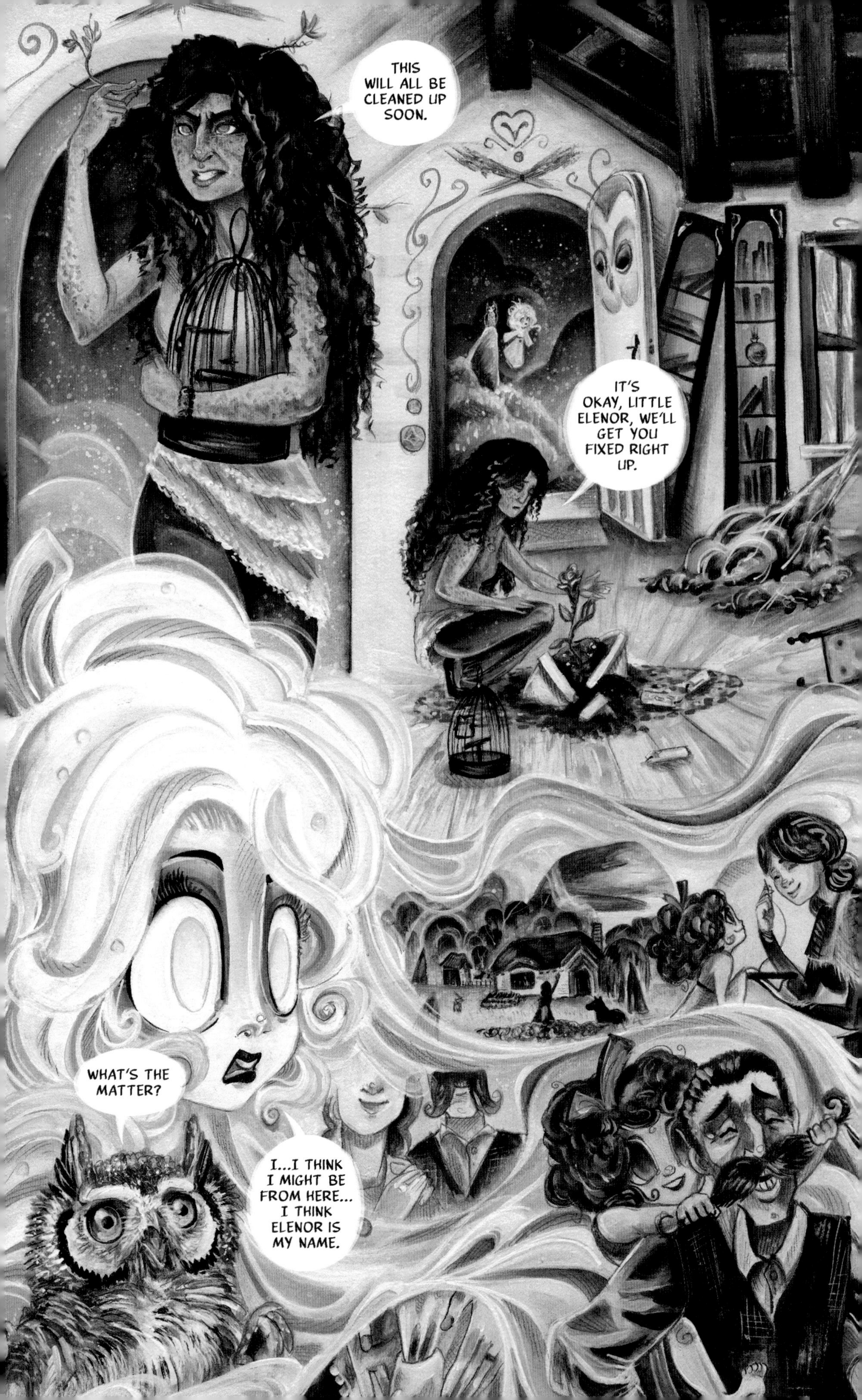
THIS WILL ALL BE CLEANED UP SOON.
IT'S OKAY, LITTLE ELENOR, WE'LL GET YOU FIXED RIGHT UP.
WHAT'S THE MATTER?
I...I THINK I MIGHT BE FROM HERE... I THINK ELENOR IS MY NAME.

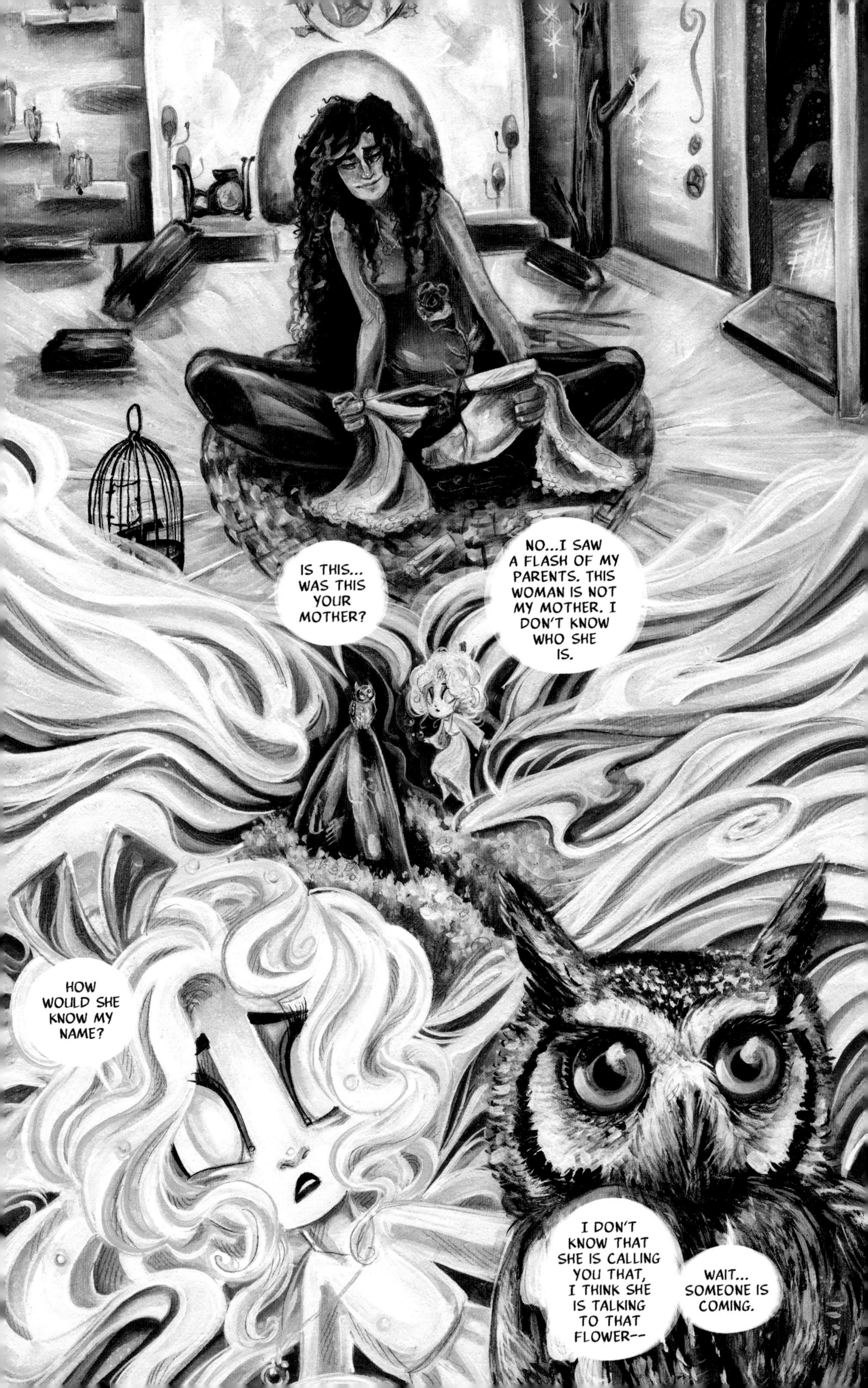
IS THIS... WAS THIS YOUR MOTHER?
NO...I SAW A FLASH OF MY PARENTS. THIS WOMAN IS NOT MY MOTHER. I DON'T KNOW WHO SHE IS.
HOW WOULD SHE KNOW MY NAME?
I DON'T KNOW THAT SHE IS CALLING YOU THAT, I THINK SHE IS TALKING TO THAT FLOWER--
WAIT... SOMEONE IS COMING.

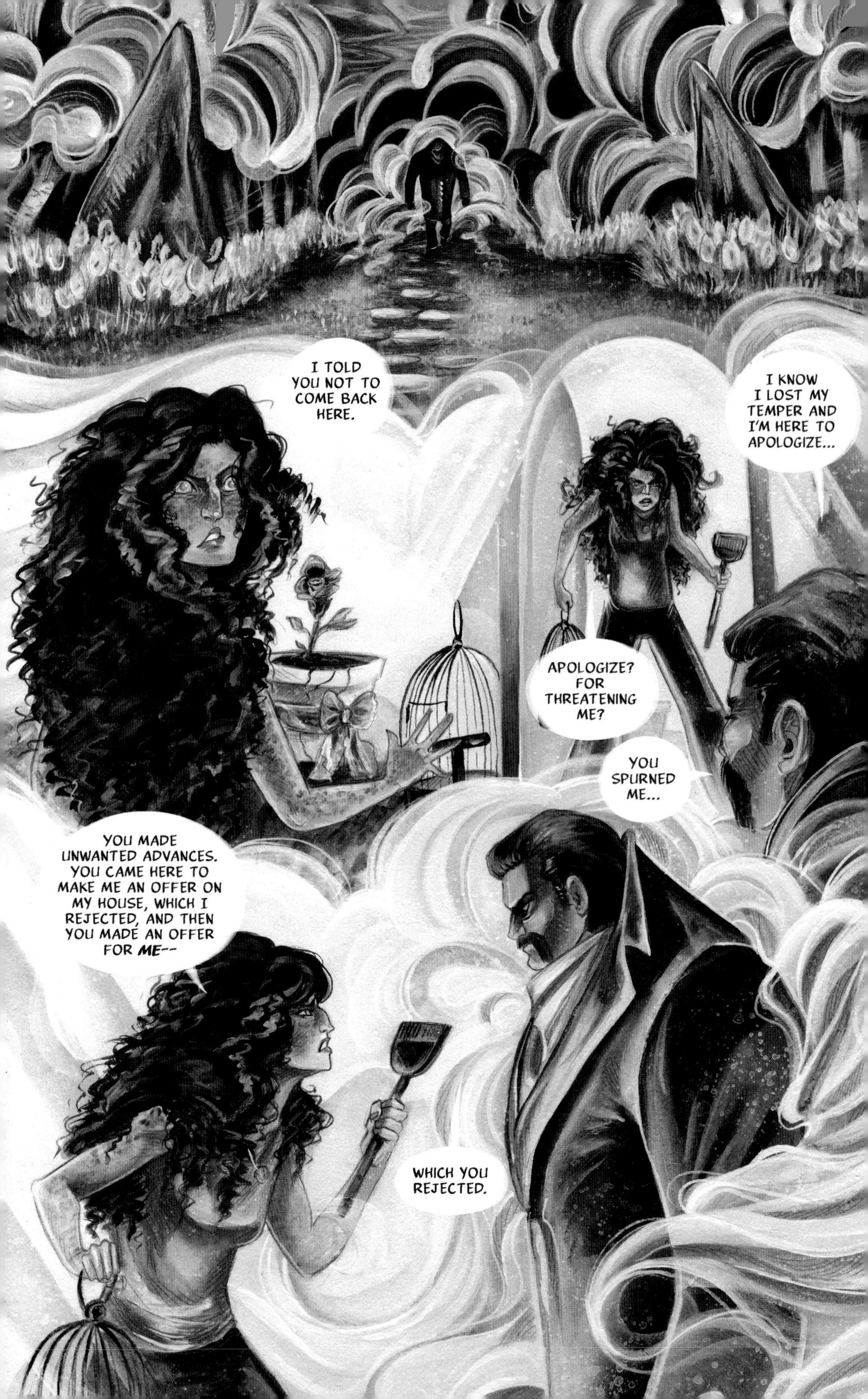
I TOLD YOU NOT TO COME BACK HERE.
I KNOW I LOST MY TEMPER AND I'M HERE TO APOLOGIZE...
APOLOGIZE? FOR THREATENING ME?
YOU SPURNED ME...
YOU MADE UNWANTED ADVANCES. YOU CAME HERE TO MAKE ME AN OFFER ON MY HOUSE, WHICH I REJECTED, AND THEN YOU MADE AN OFFER FOR *ME*--
WHICH YOU REJECTED.

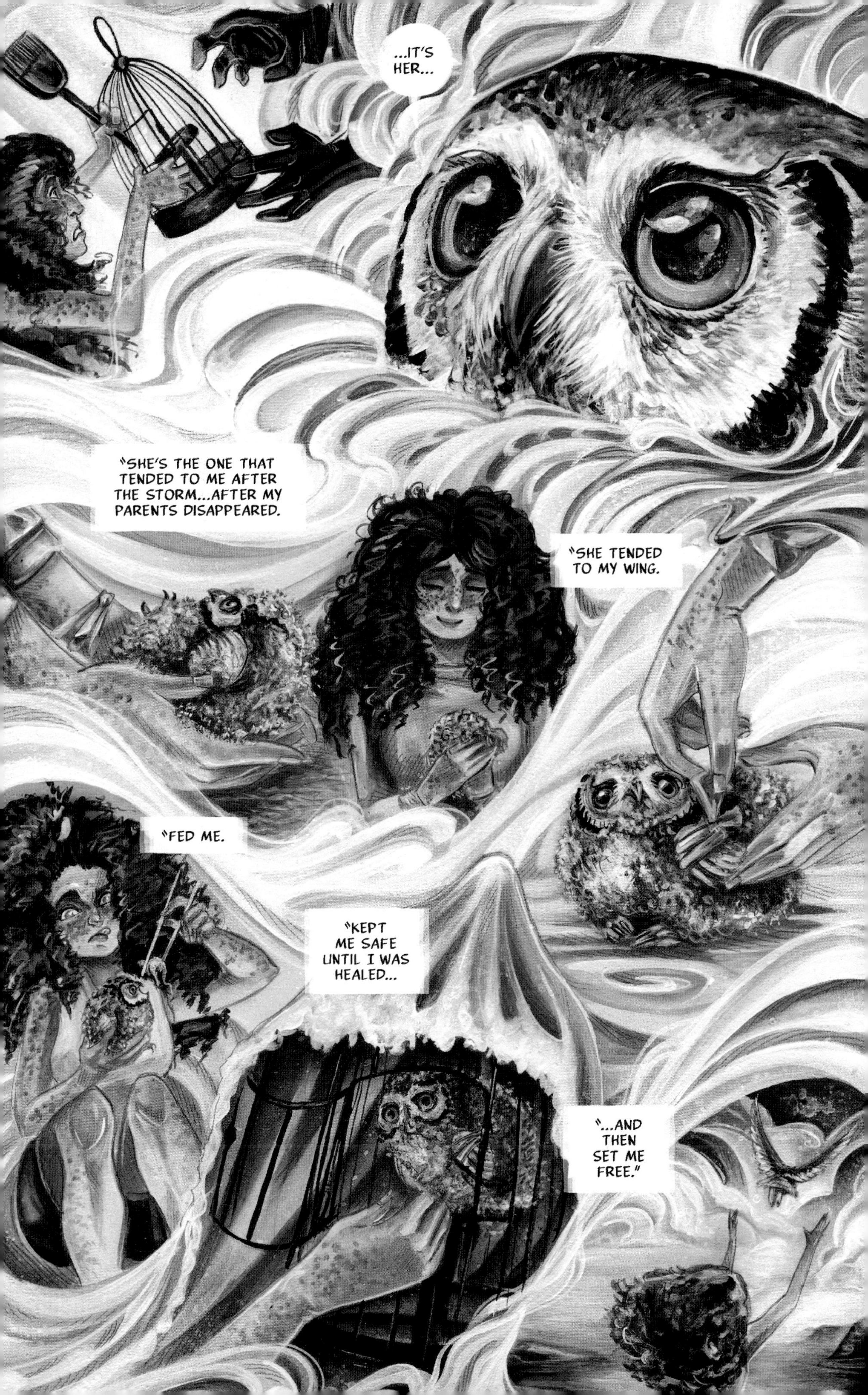
...IT'S HER...
"SHE'S THE ONE THAT TENDED TO ME AFTER THE STORM...AFTER MY PARENTS DISAPPEARED.
"SHE TENDED TO MY WING.
"FED ME.
"KEPT ME SAFE UNTIL I WAS HEALED...
"...AND THEN SET ME FREE."

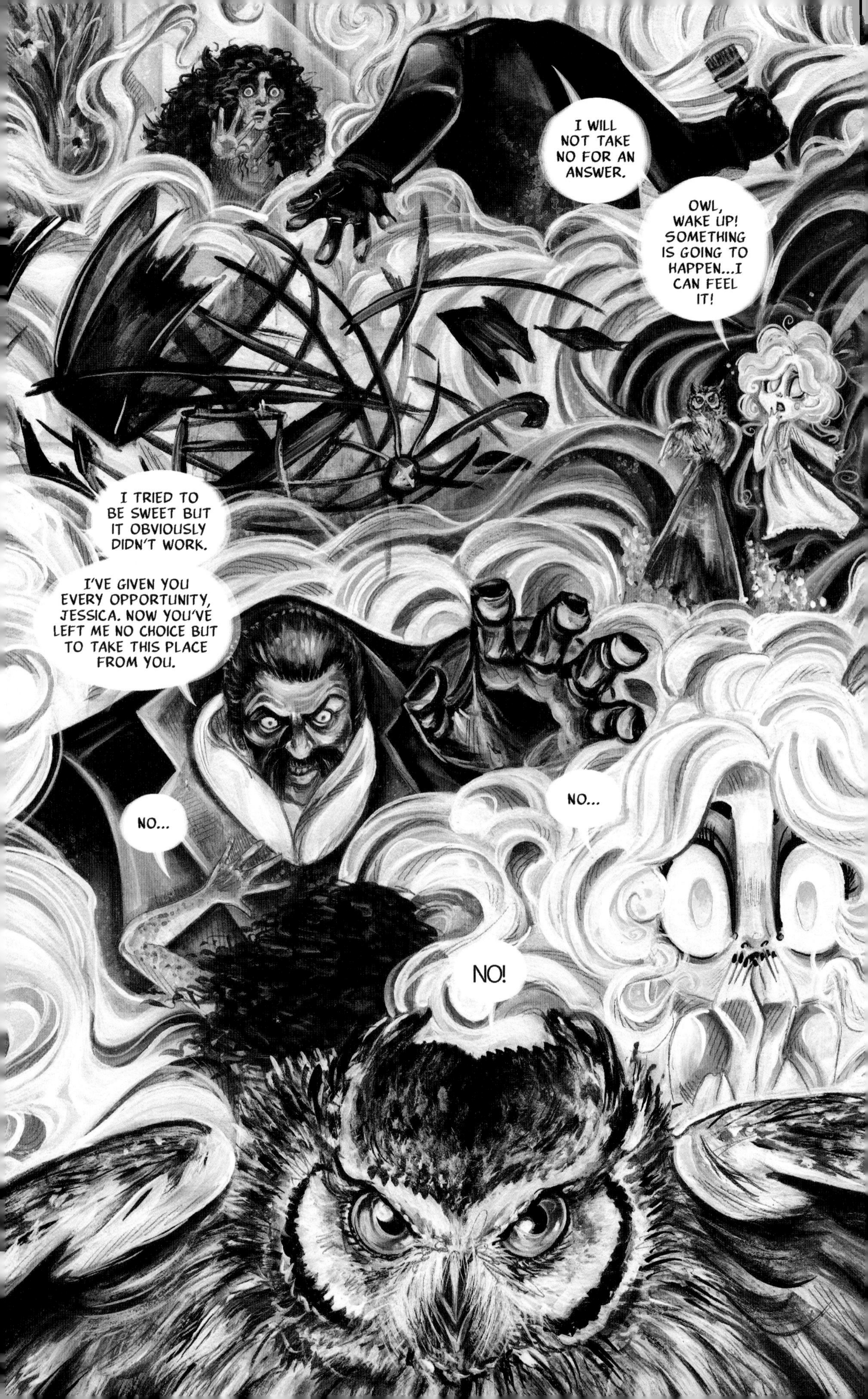
I WILL NOT TAKE NO FOR AN ANSWER.
OWL, WAKE UP! SOMETHING IS GOING TO HAPPEN...I CAN FEEL IT!
I TRIED TO BE SWEET BUT IT OBVIOUSLY DIDN'T WORK.
I'VE GIVEN YOU EVERY OPPORTUNITY, JESSICA. NOW YOU'VE LEFT ME NO CHOICE BUT TO TAKE THIS PLACE FROM YOU.
NO...
NO...
NO!

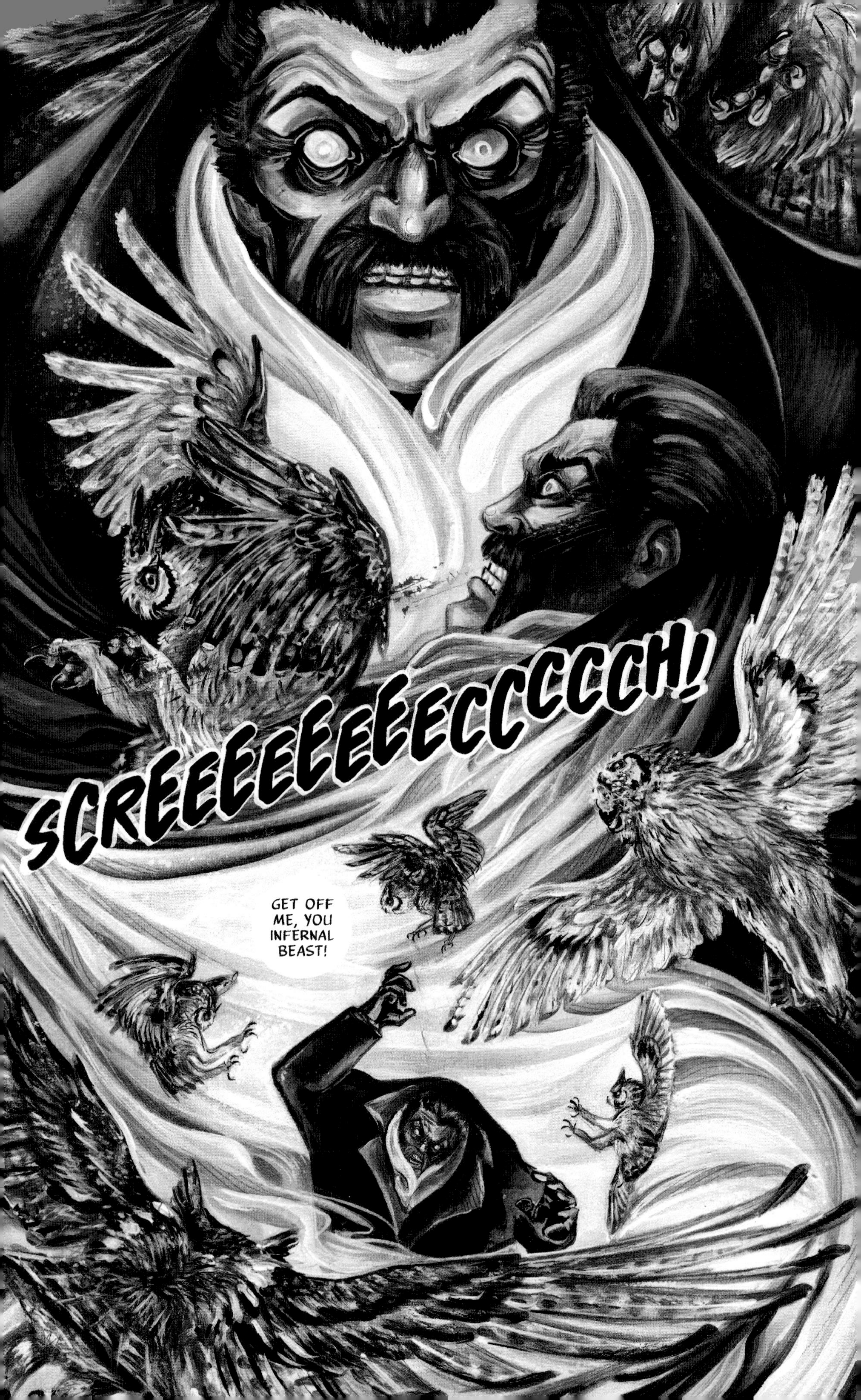
SCREEEEEEEEECCCCCH!
GET OFF ME, YOU INFERNAL BEAST!

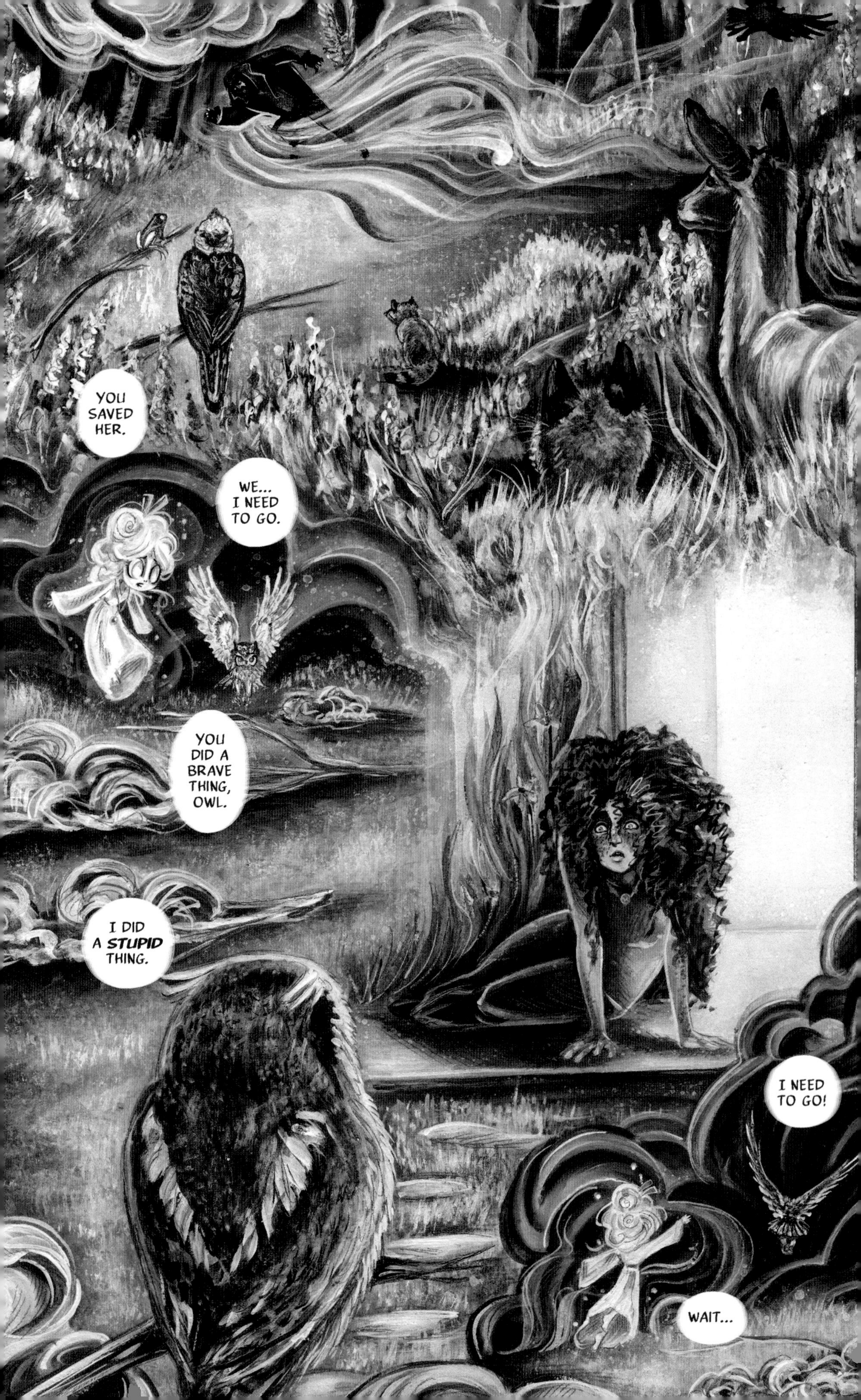
YOU SAVED HER.
WE... I NEED TO GO.
YOU DID A BRAVE THING, OWL.
I DID A **STUPID** THING.
I NEED TO GO!
WAIT...

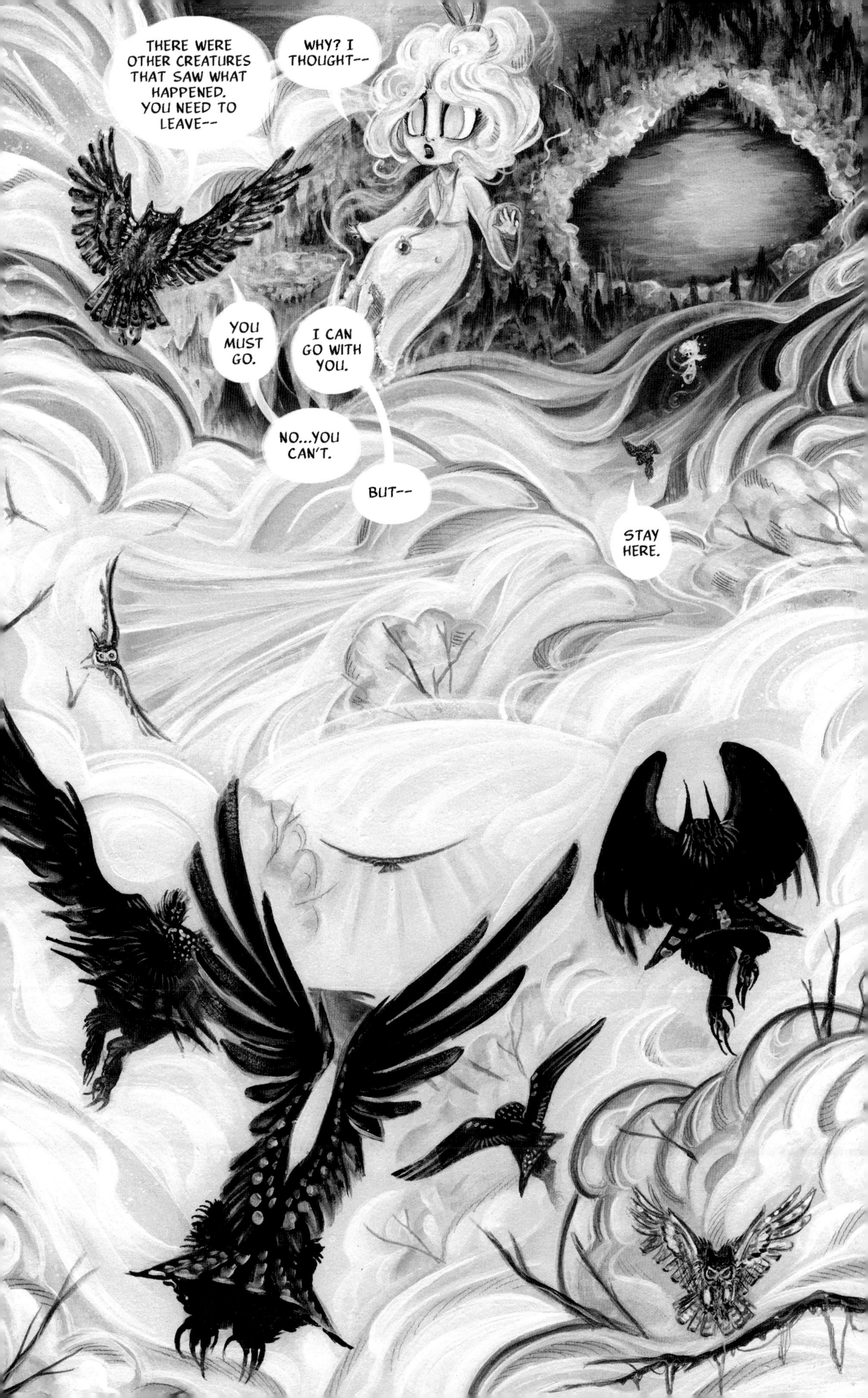
THERE WERE OTHER CREATURES THAT SAW WHAT HAPPENED. YOU NEED TO LEAVE--
WHY? I THOUGHT--
YOU MUST GO.
I CAN GO WITH YOU.
NO...YOU CAN'T.
BUT--
STAY HERE.

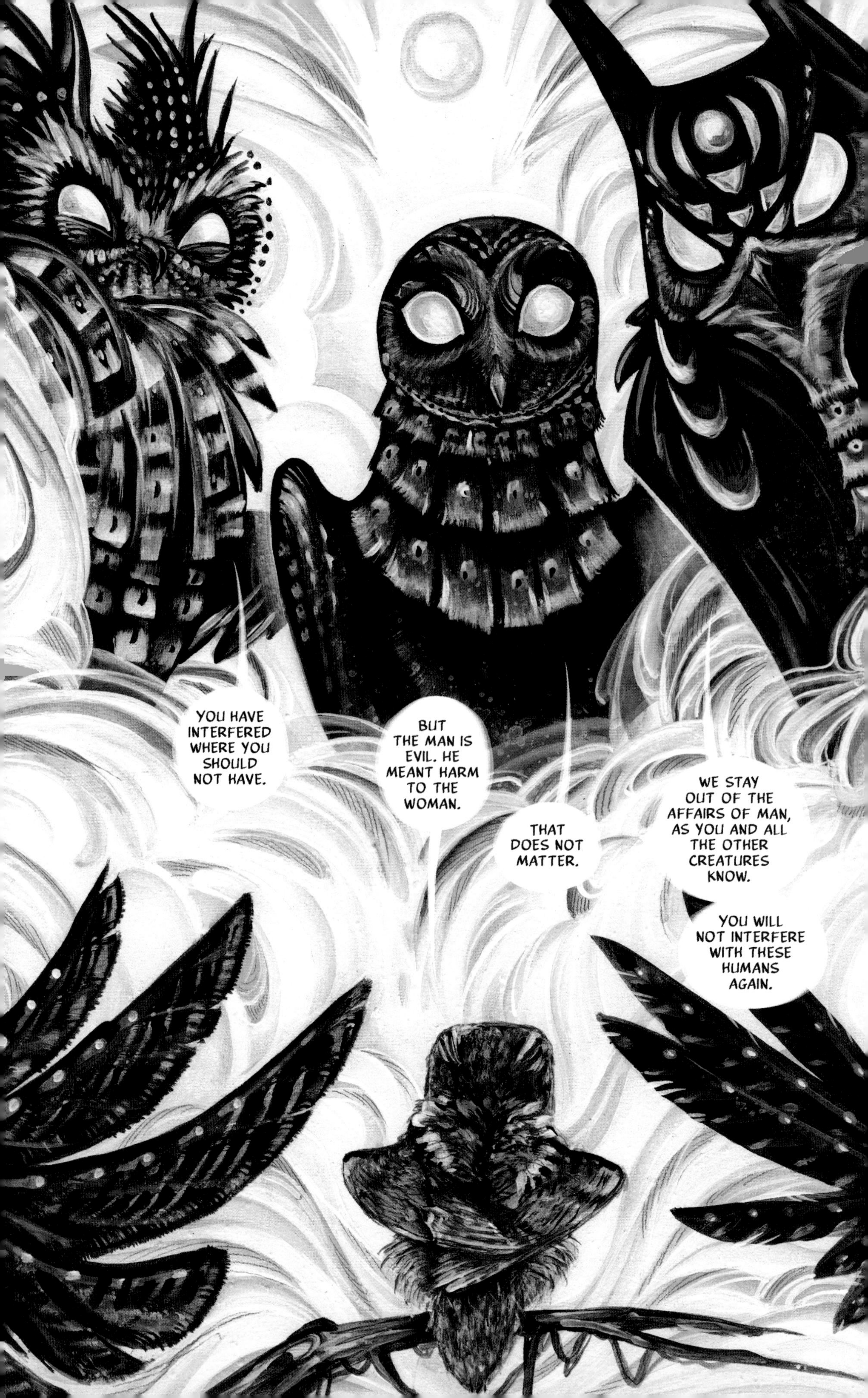
YOU HAVE INTERFERED WHERE YOU SHOULD NOT HAVE.
BUT THE MAN IS EVIL. HE MEANT HARM TO THE WOMAN.
THAT DOES NOT MATTER.
WE STAY OUT OF THE AFFAIRS OF MAN, AS YOU AND ALL THE OTHER CREATURES KNOW.
YOU WILL NOT INTERFERE WITH THESE HUMANS AGAIN.

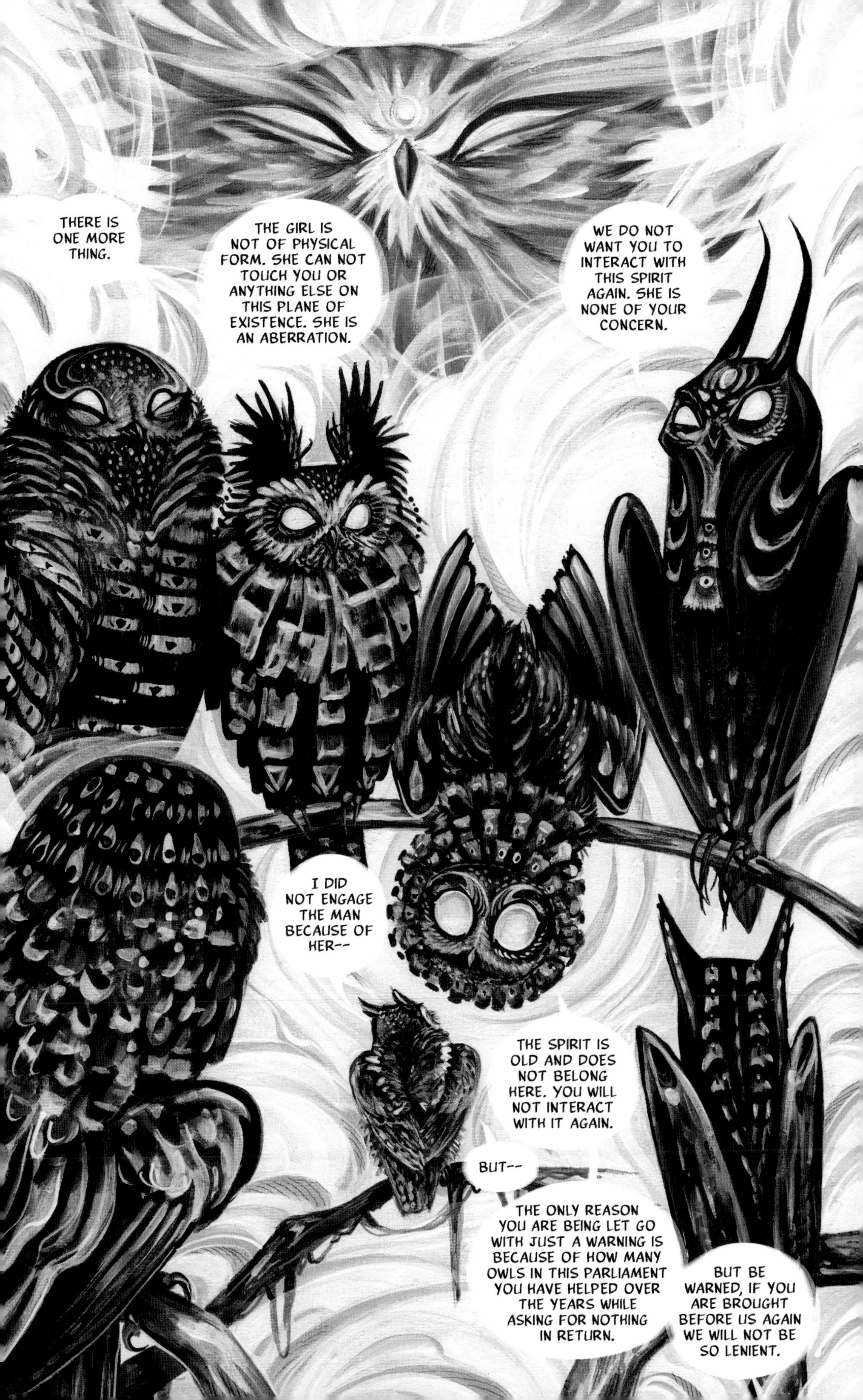
THERE IS ONE MORE THING.
THE GIRL IS NOT OF PHYSICAL FORM. SHE CAN NOT TOUCH YOU OR ANYTHING ELSE ON THIS PLANE OF EXISTENCE. SHE IS AN ABERRATION.
WE DO NOT WANT YOU TO INTERACT WITH THIS SPIRIT AGAIN. SHE IS NONE OF YOUR CONCERN.
I DID NOT ENGAGE THE MAN BECAUSE OF HER--
THE SPIRIT IS OLD AND DOES NOT BELONG HERE. YOU WILL NOT INTERACT WITH IT AGAIN.
BUT--
THE ONLY REASON YOU ARE BEING LET GO WITH JUST A WARNING IS BECAUSE OF HOW MANY OWLS IN THIS PARLIAMENT YOU HAVE HELPED OVER THE YEARS WHILE ASKING FOR NOTHING IN RETURN.
BUT BE WARNED, IF YOU ARE BROUGHT BEFORE US AGAIN WE WILL NOT BE SO LENIENT.

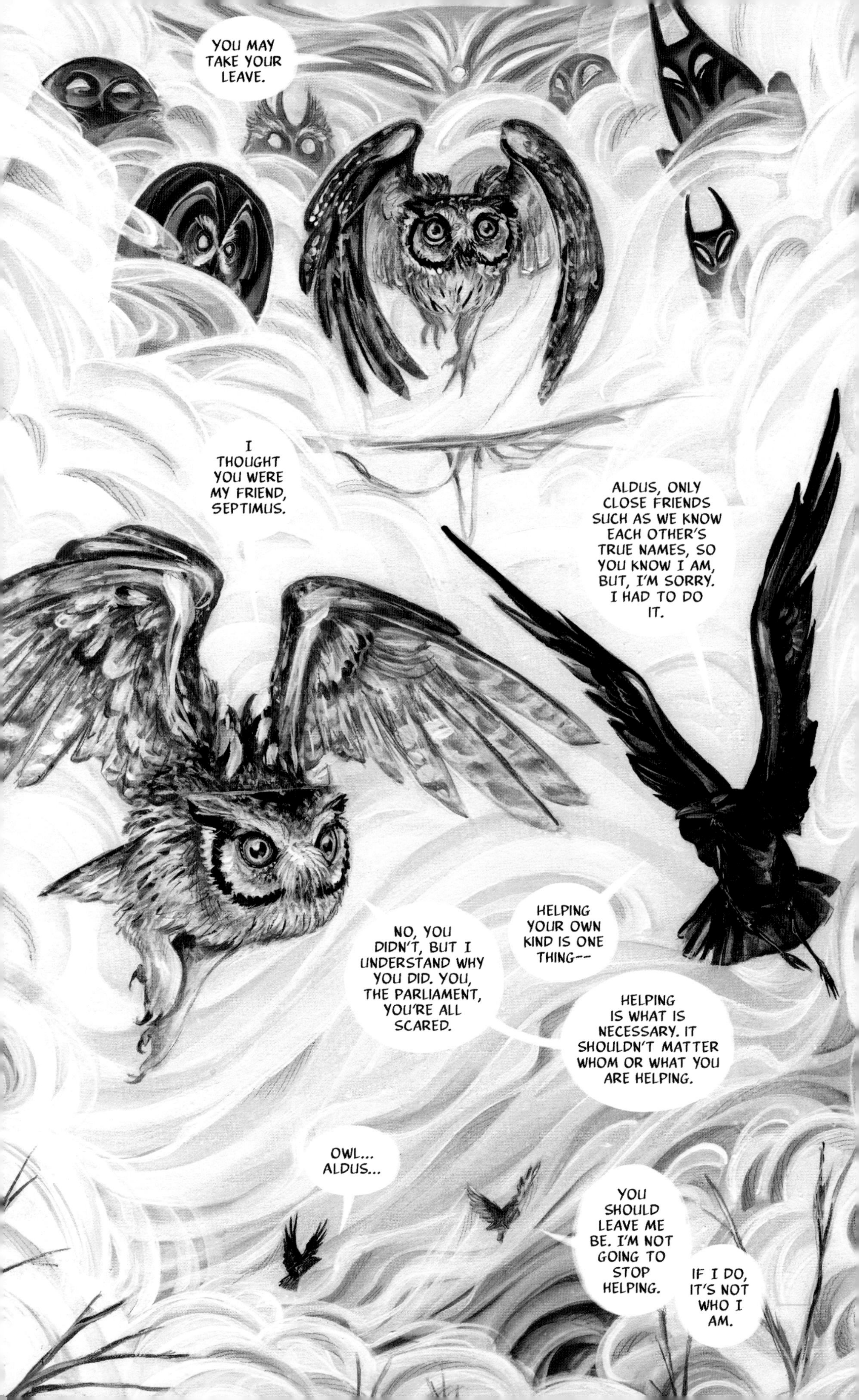
YOU MAY TAKE YOUR LEAVE.
I THOUGHT YOU WERE MY FRIEND, SEPTIMUS.
ALDUS, ONLY CLOSE FRIENDS SUCH AS WE KNOW EACH OTHER'S TRUE NAMES, SO YOU KNOW I AM, BUT, I'M SORRY. I HAD TO DO IT.
NO, YOU DIDN'T, BUT I UNDERSTAND WHY YOU DID. YOU, THE PARLIAMENT, YOU'RE ALL SCARED.
HELPING YOUR OWN KIND IS ONE THING--
HELPING IS WHAT IS NECESSARY. IT SHOULDN'T MATTER WHOM OR WHAT YOU ARE HELPING.
OWL... ALDUS...
YOU SHOULD LEAVE ME BE. I'M NOT GOING TO STOP HELPING.
IF I DO, IT'S NOT WHO I AM.

SHE IS NOT HERE ALDUS.
SHE MUST HAVE GONE BACK TO THE WOMAN AND THE HOUSE--
I ASKED YOU TO LEAVE ME BE, CROW.
THERE'S SOMETHING ELSE. OTHERS HAVE JUST TOLD ME THE MAN IS ON HIS WAY BACK.
HE'S GOING BACK TO THE WOMAN.
ALDUS... THERE'S A GREAT DEAL OF CHATTER. HE'S CARRYING THE STORM.
WHAT?
SEPTIMUS! WARN EVERYONE!

THERE, THERE, LITTLE FLOWER, YOU JUST NEED SOME WATER TO BRING YOU BACK TO LIFE.
WHAT IS MY CONNECTION TO YOU?
YOU ARE NOT MY MOTHER...
...BUT I AM CONNECTED TO YOU SOMEHOW.
PLEASE, I WANT TO KNOW...
WHAT?
WHAT IS IT?

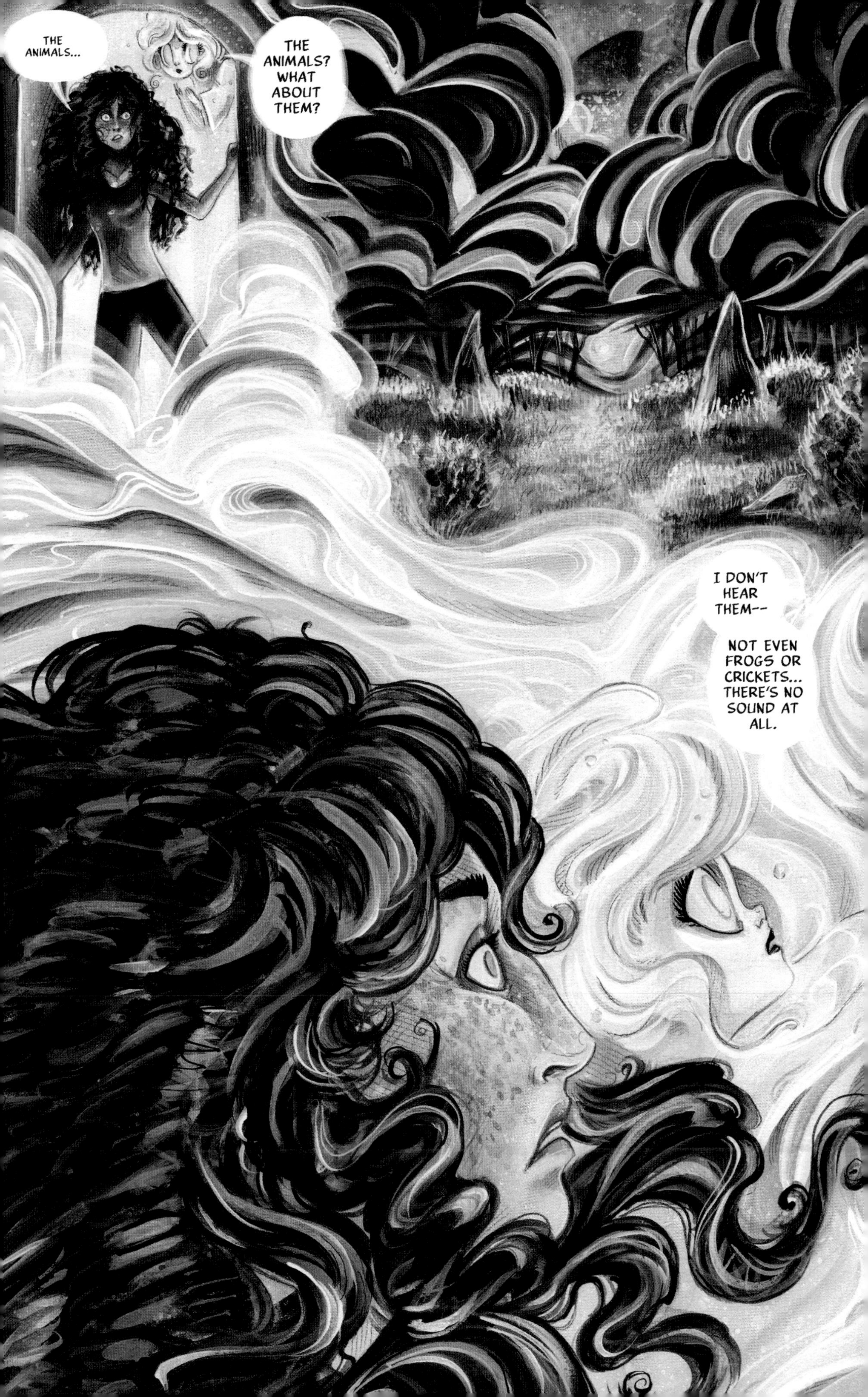
THE ANIMALS...
THE ANIMALS? WHAT ABOUT THEM?
I DON'T HEAR THEM--
NOT EVEN FROGS OR CRICKETS... THERE'S NO SOUND AT ALL.

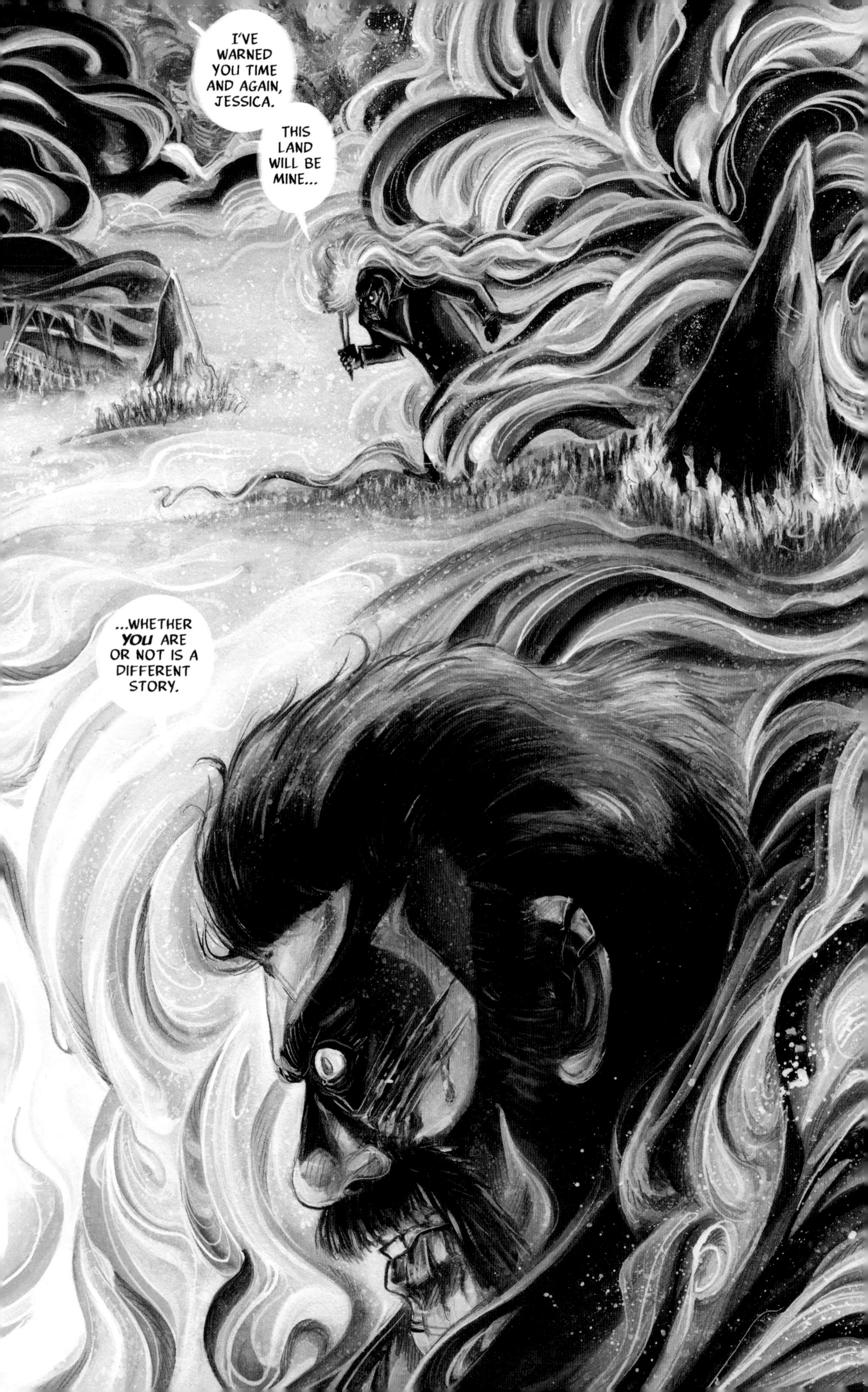
I'VE WARNED YOU TIME AND AGAIN, JESSICA.
THIS LAND WILL BE MINE...
...WHETHER YOU ARE OR NOT IS A DIFFERENT STORY.

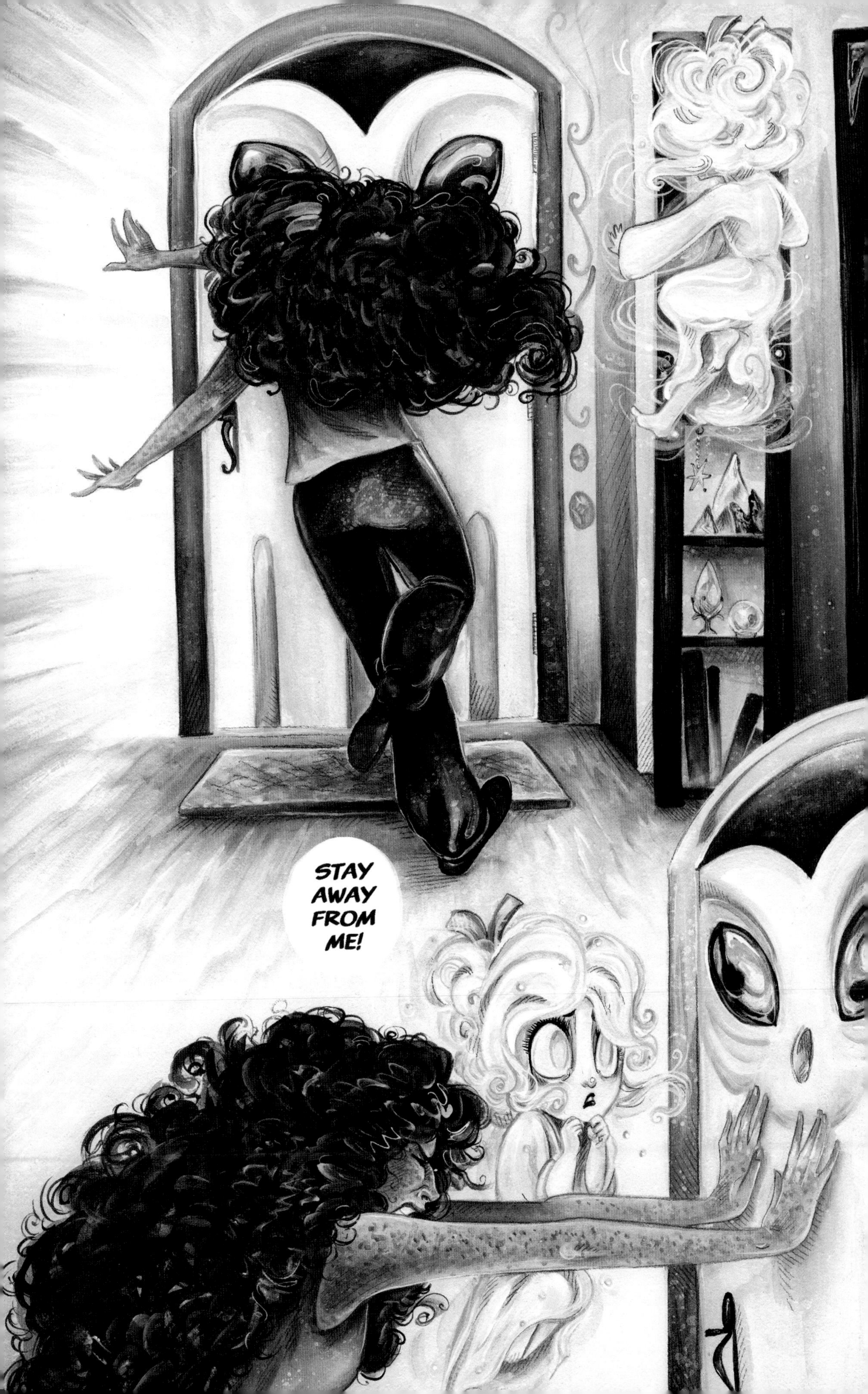
STAY AWAY FROM ME!

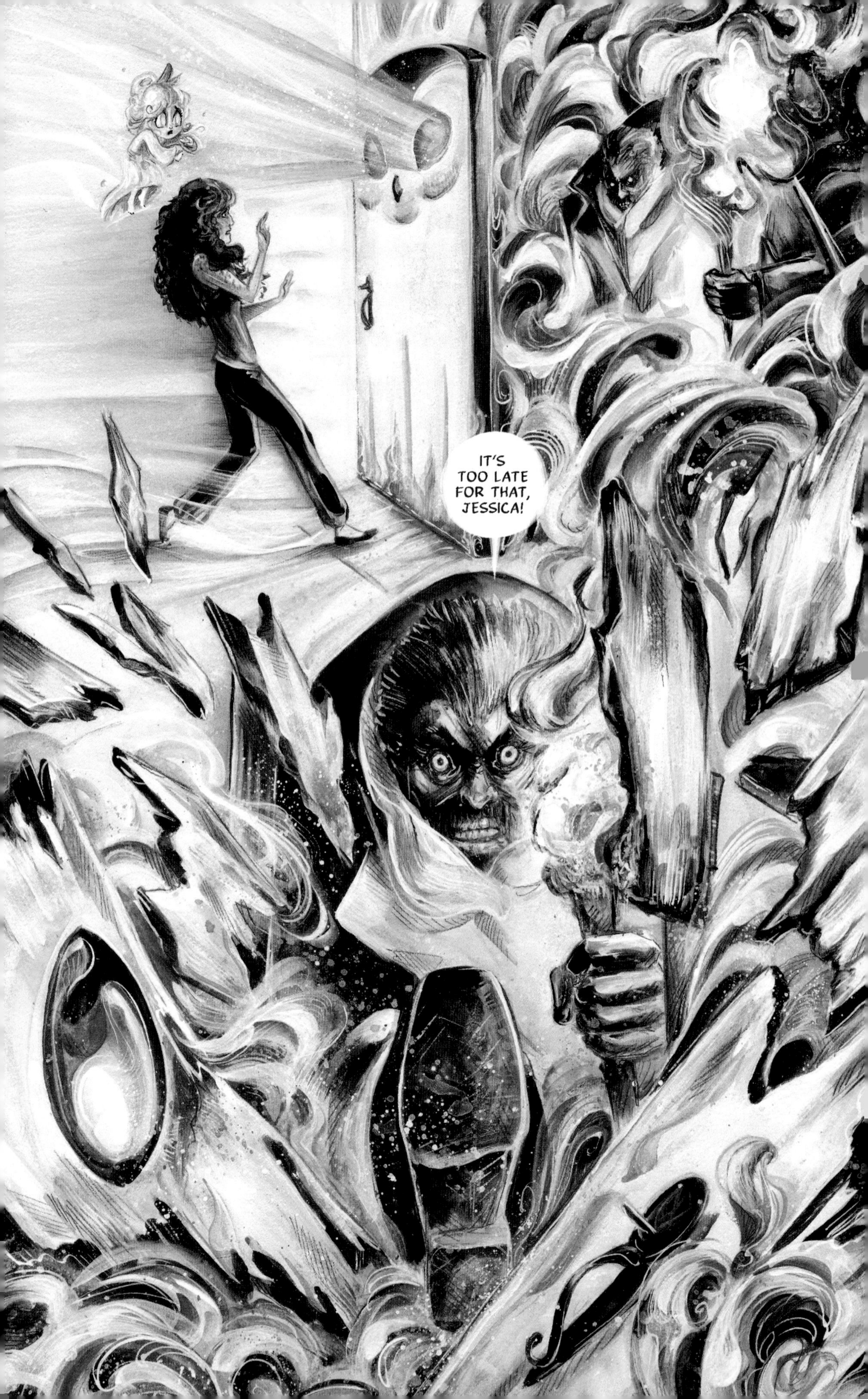
IT'S TOO LATE FOR THAT, JESSICA!

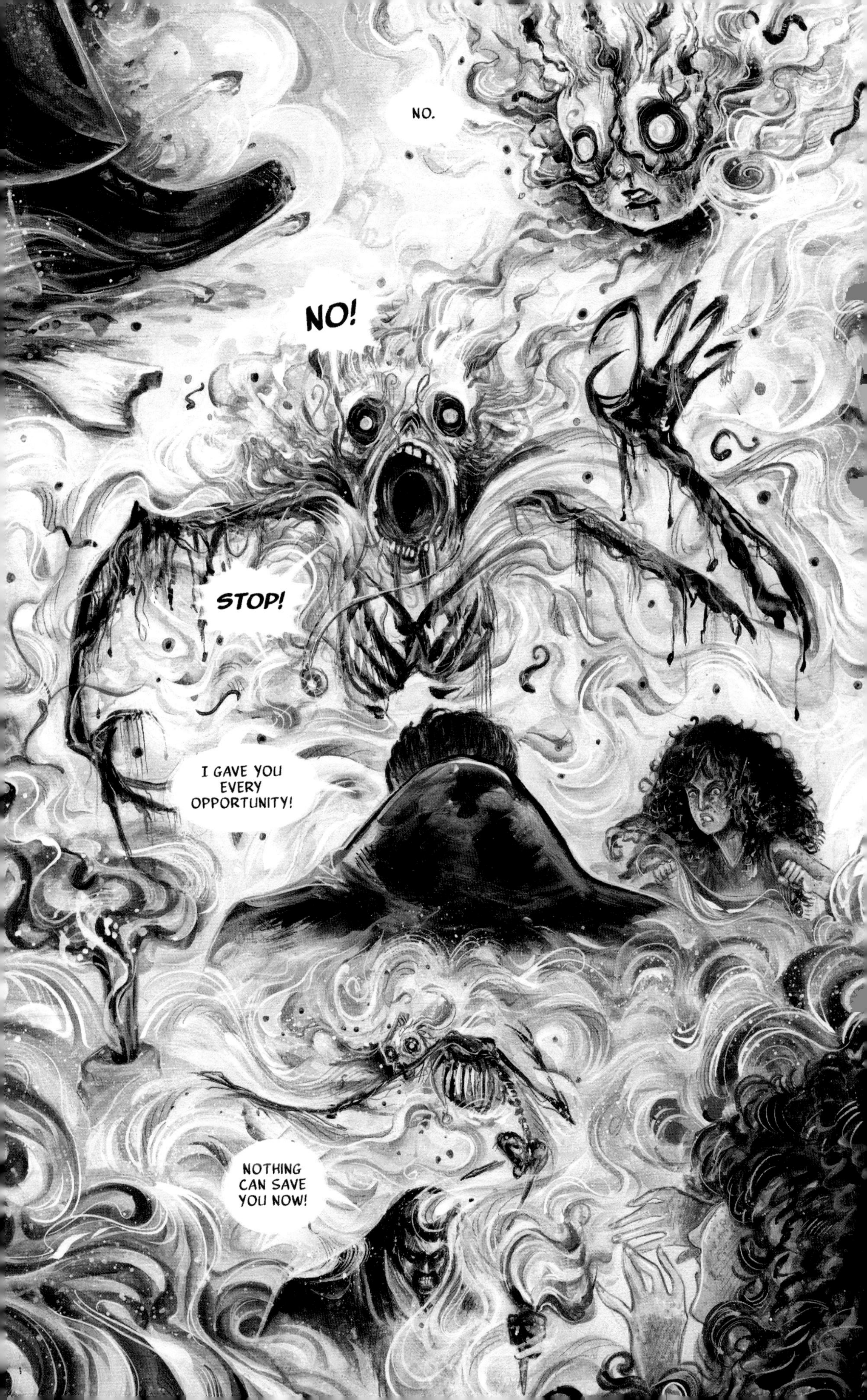
NO.
NO!
STOP!
I GAVE YOU EVERY OPPORTUNITY!
NOTHING CAN SAVE YOU NOW!

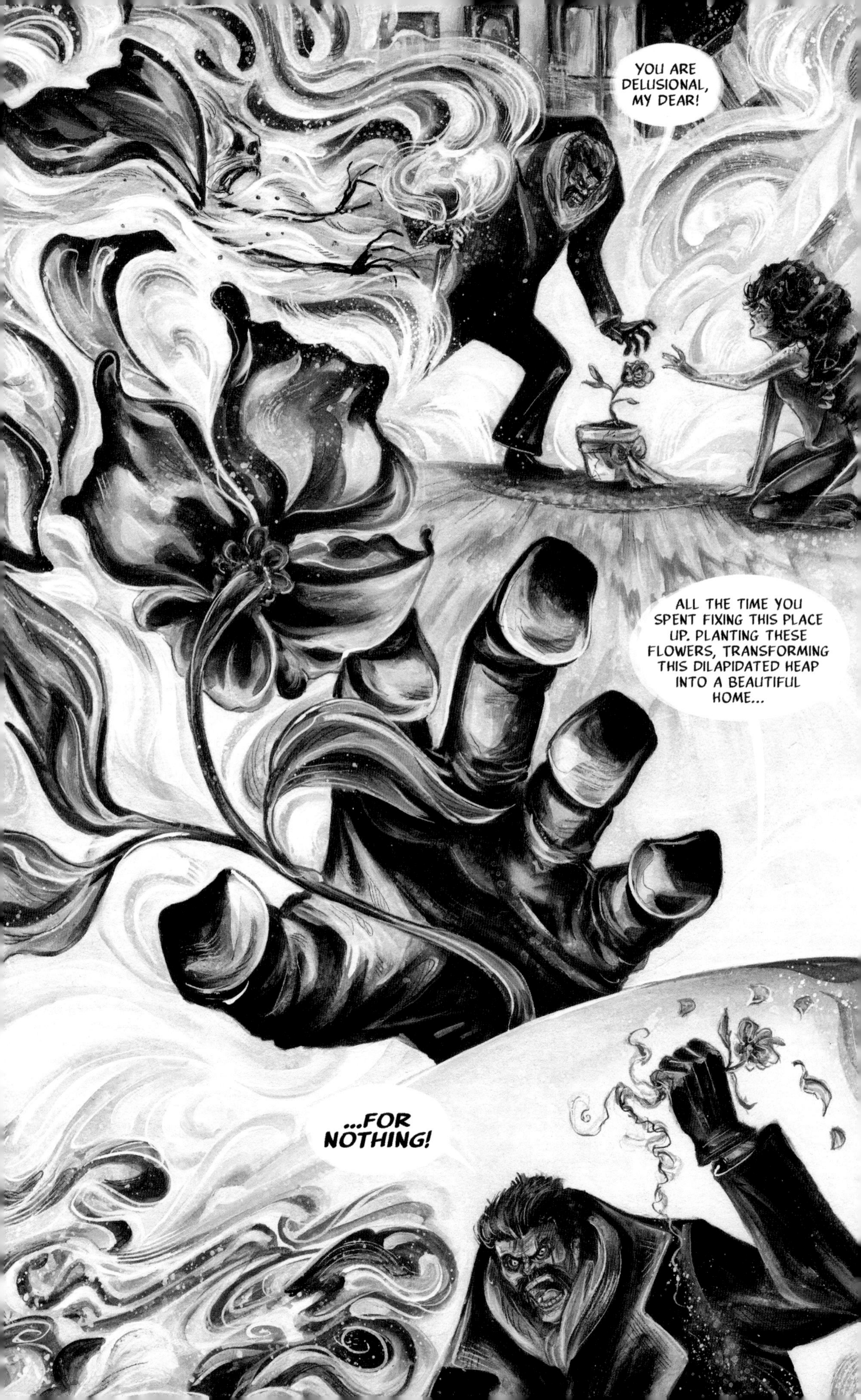
YOU ARE DELUSIONAL, MY DEAR!
ALL THE TIME YOU SPENT FIXING THIS PLACE UP. PLANTING THESE FLOWERS, TRANSFORMING THIS DILAPIDATED HEAP INTO A BEAUTIFUL HOME...
...FOR NOTHING!

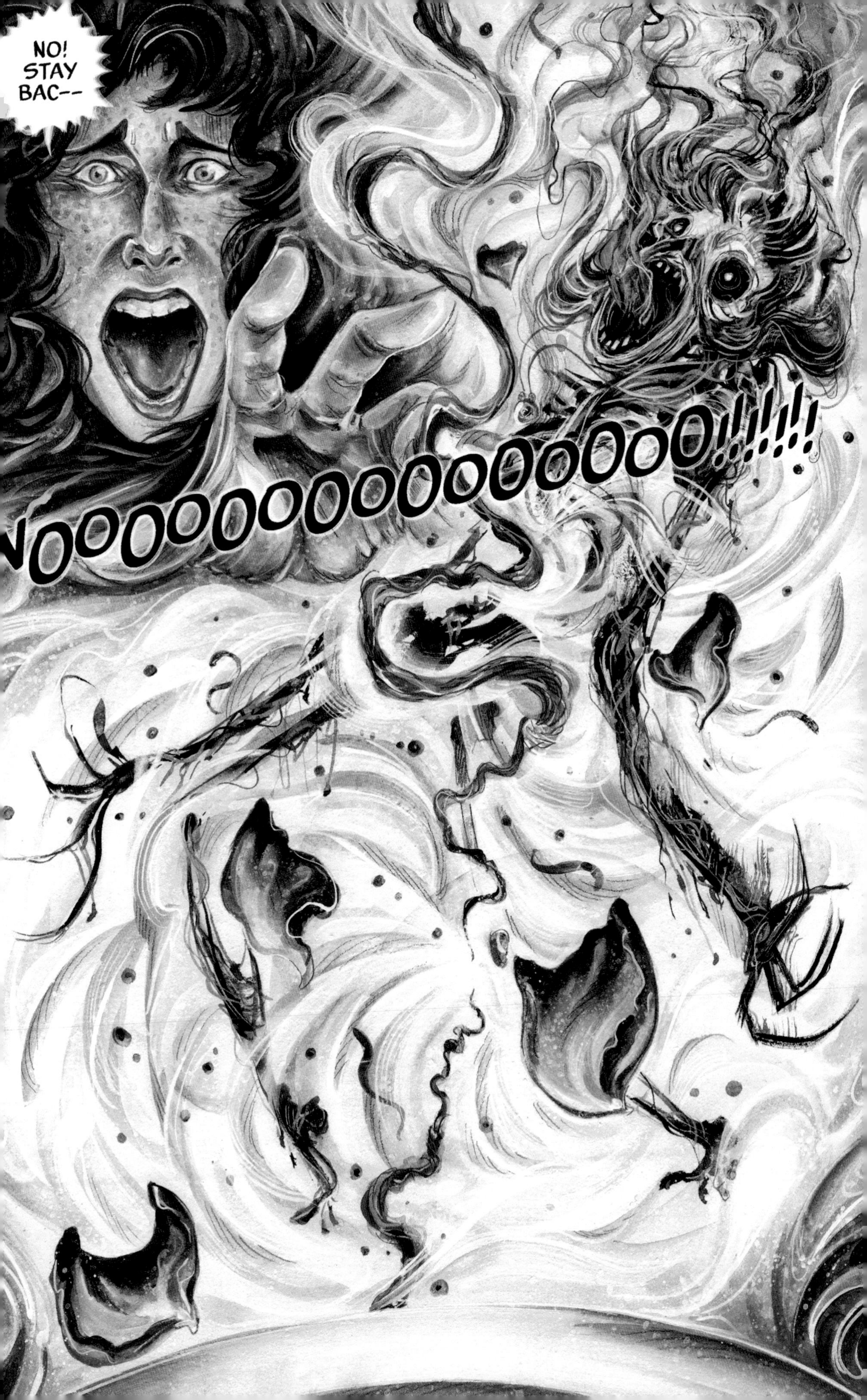
NO! STAY BAC--
NOOOOOOOOOOOOOOOOOO!!!!!!

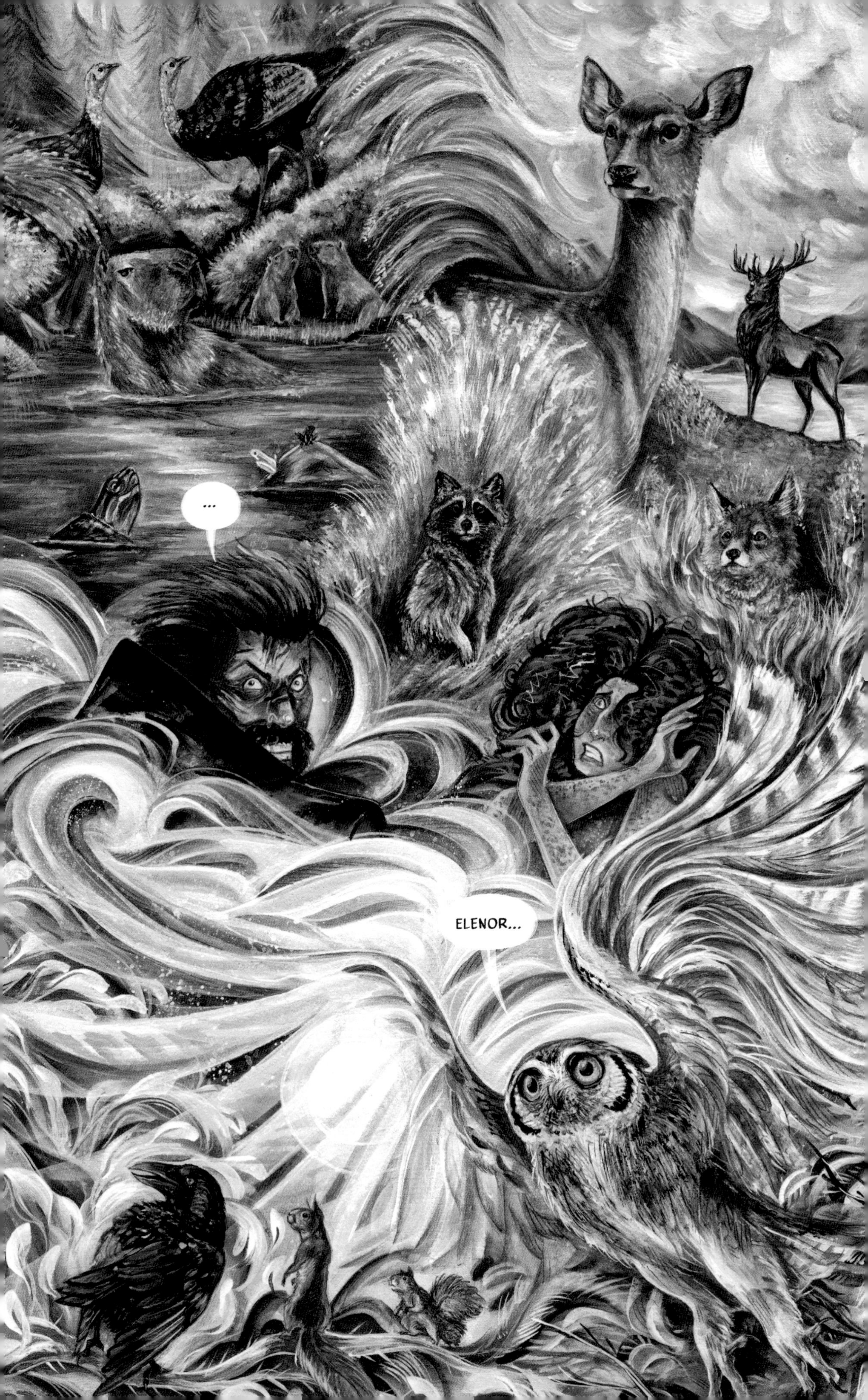
...
ELENOR...

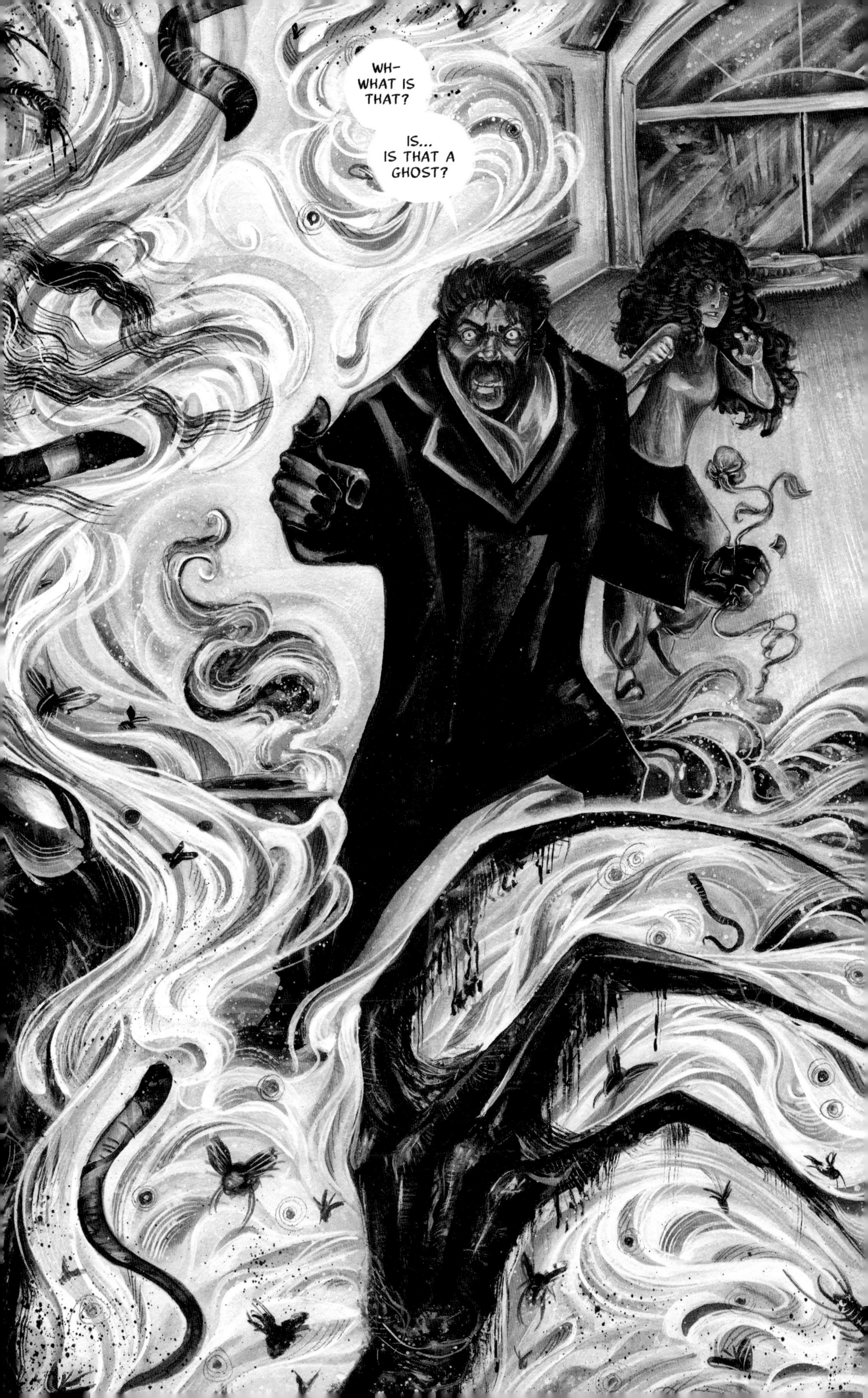
WH-
WHAT IS
THAT?
IS...
IS THAT A
GHOST?

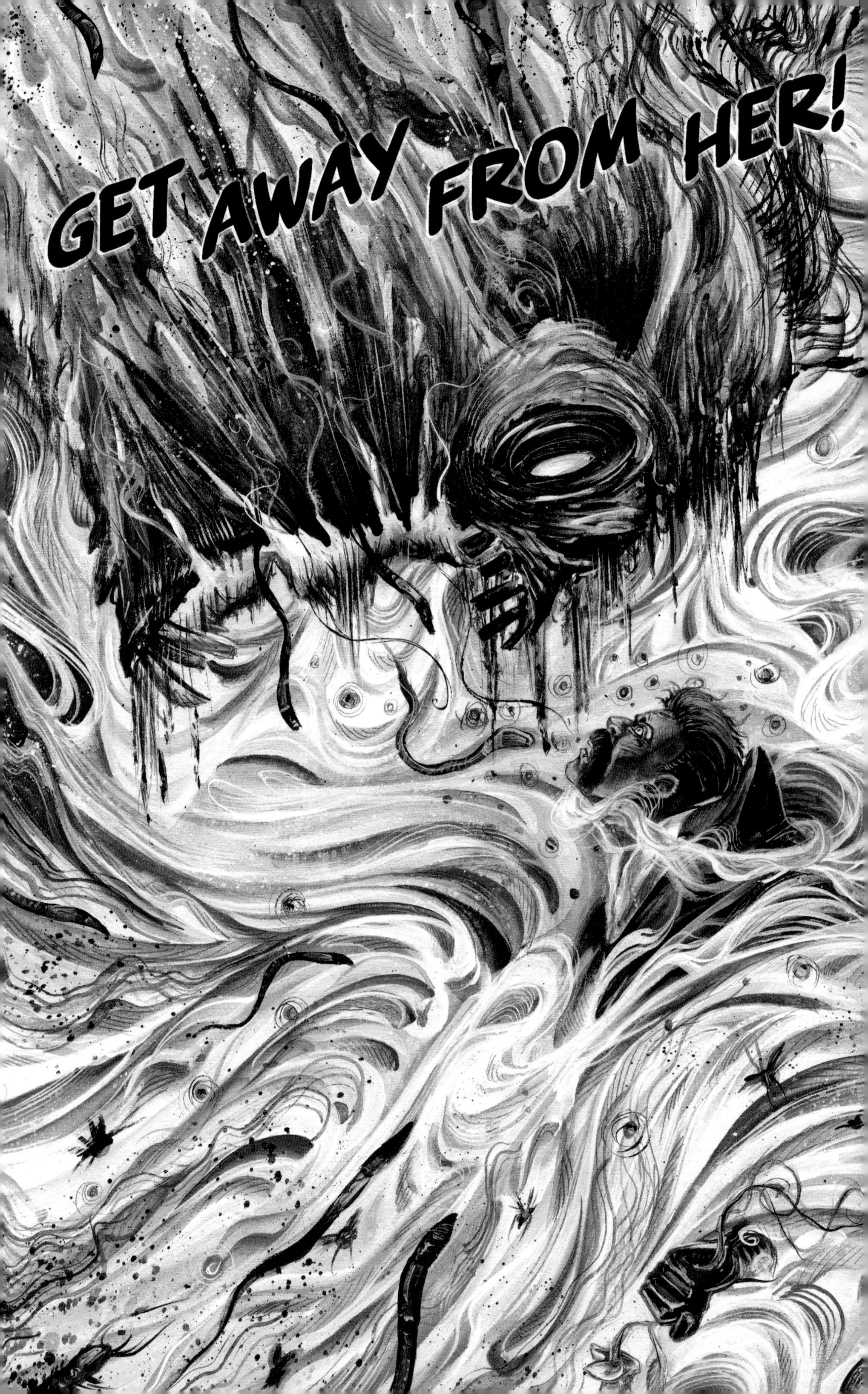
GET AWAY FROM HER!

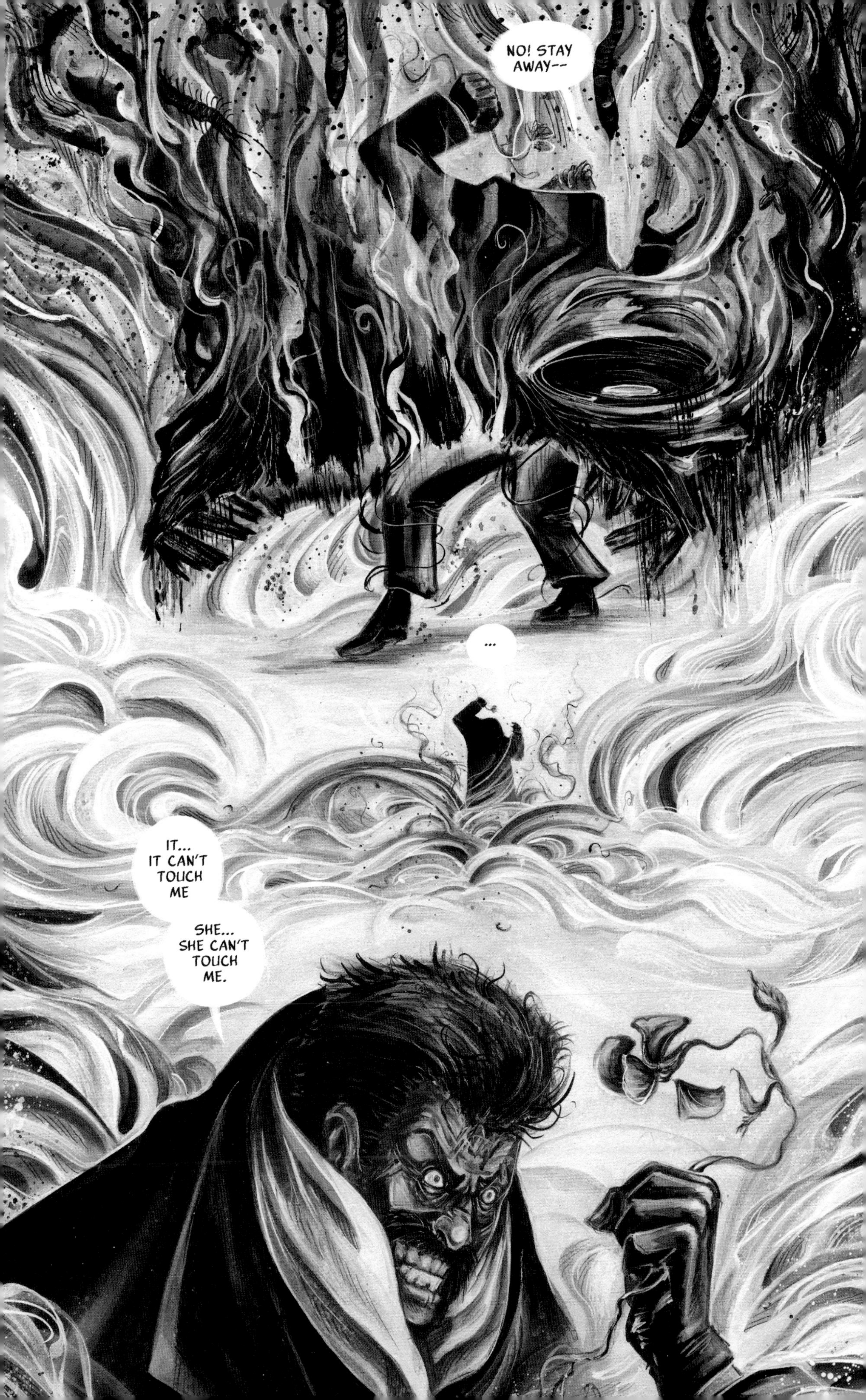
NO! STAY AWAY--
...
IT... IT CAN'T TOUCH ME
SHE... SHE CAN'T TOUCH ME.

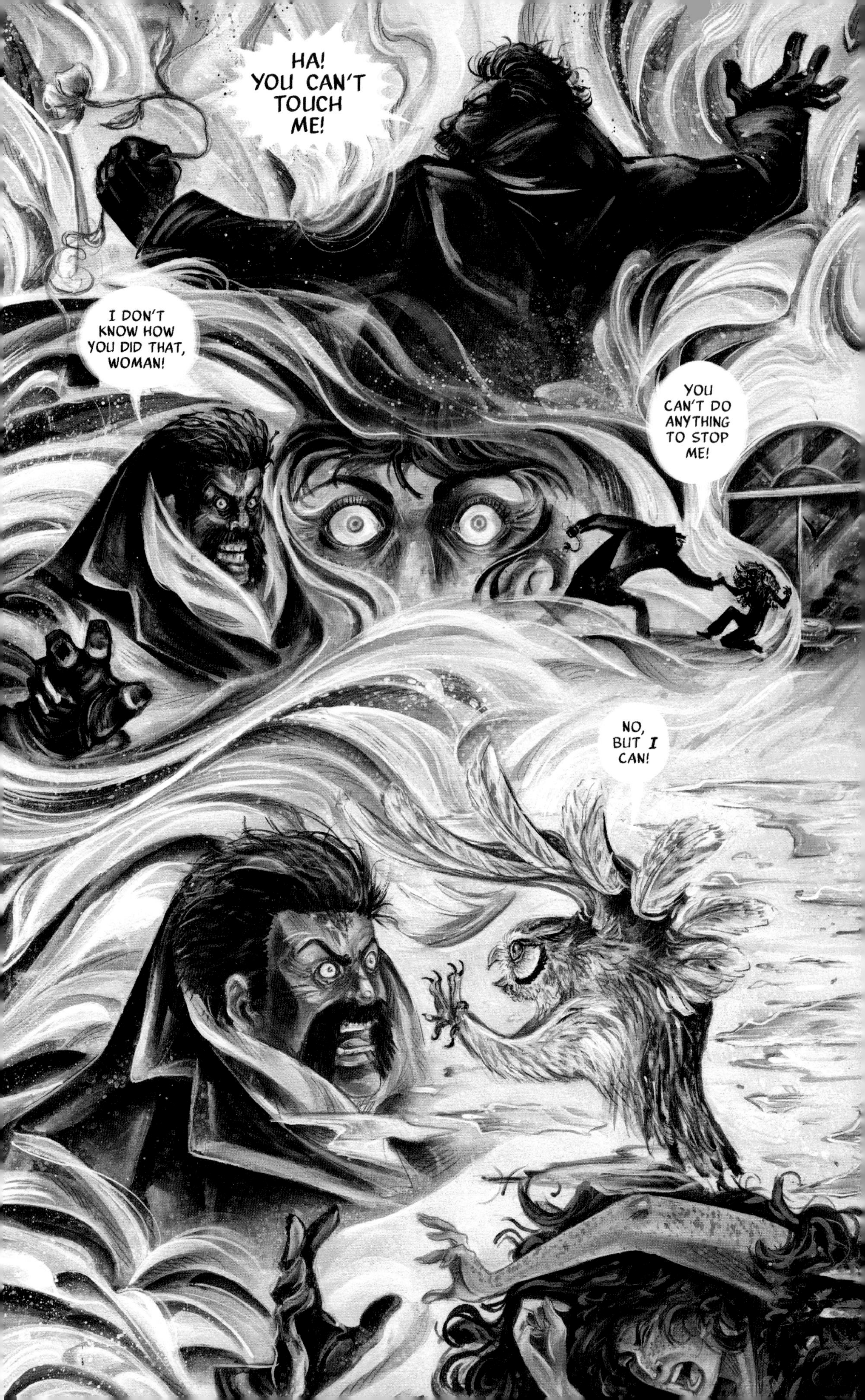
HA! YOU CAN'T TOUCH ME!
I DON'T KNOW HOW YOU DID THAT, WOMAN!
YOU CAN'T DO ANYTHING TO STOP ME!
NO, BUT I CAN!

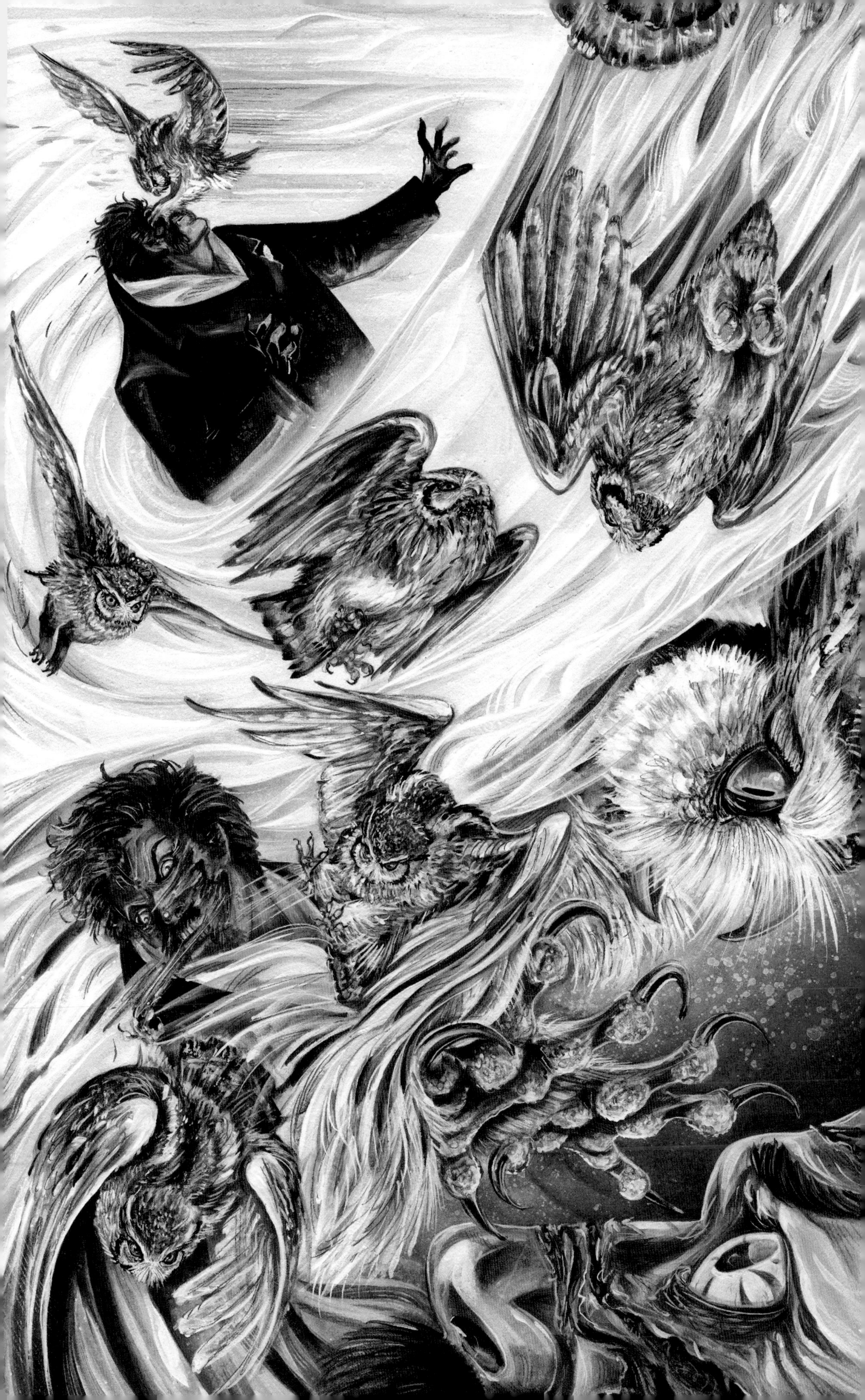

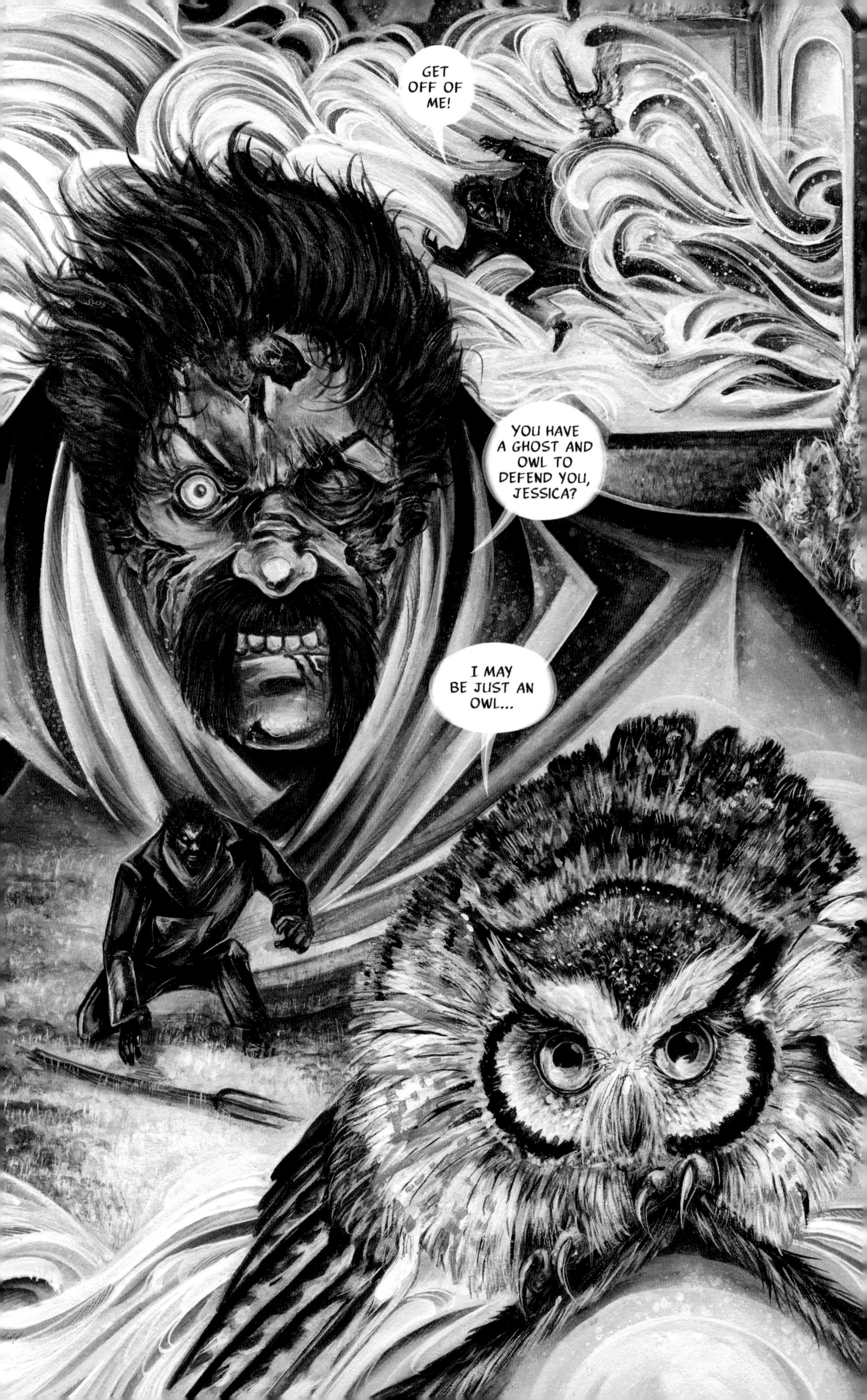
GET OFF OF ME!
YOU HAVE A GHOST AND OWL TO DEFEND YOU, JESSICA?
I MAY BE JUST AN OWL...

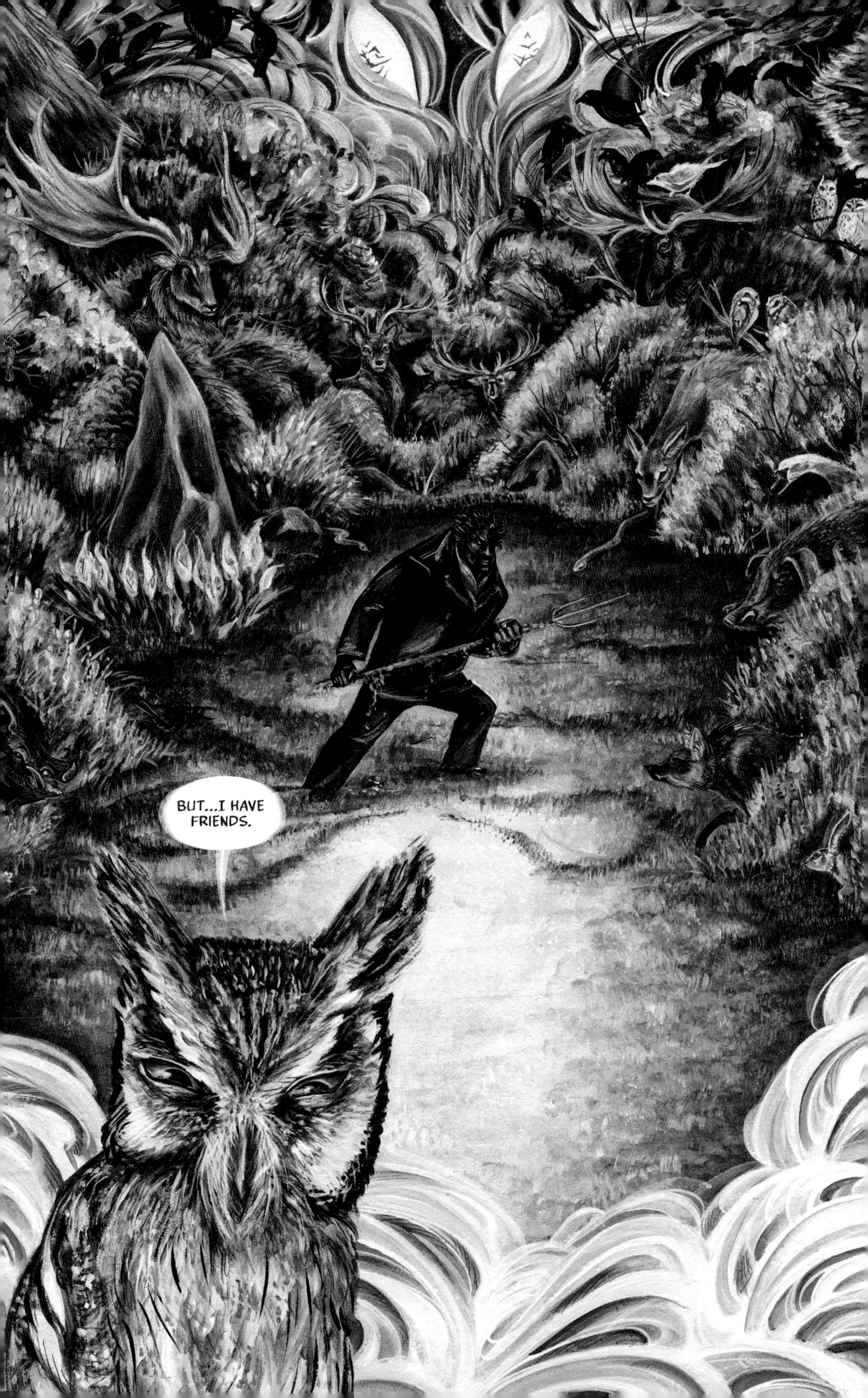
BUT...I HAVE FRIENDS.

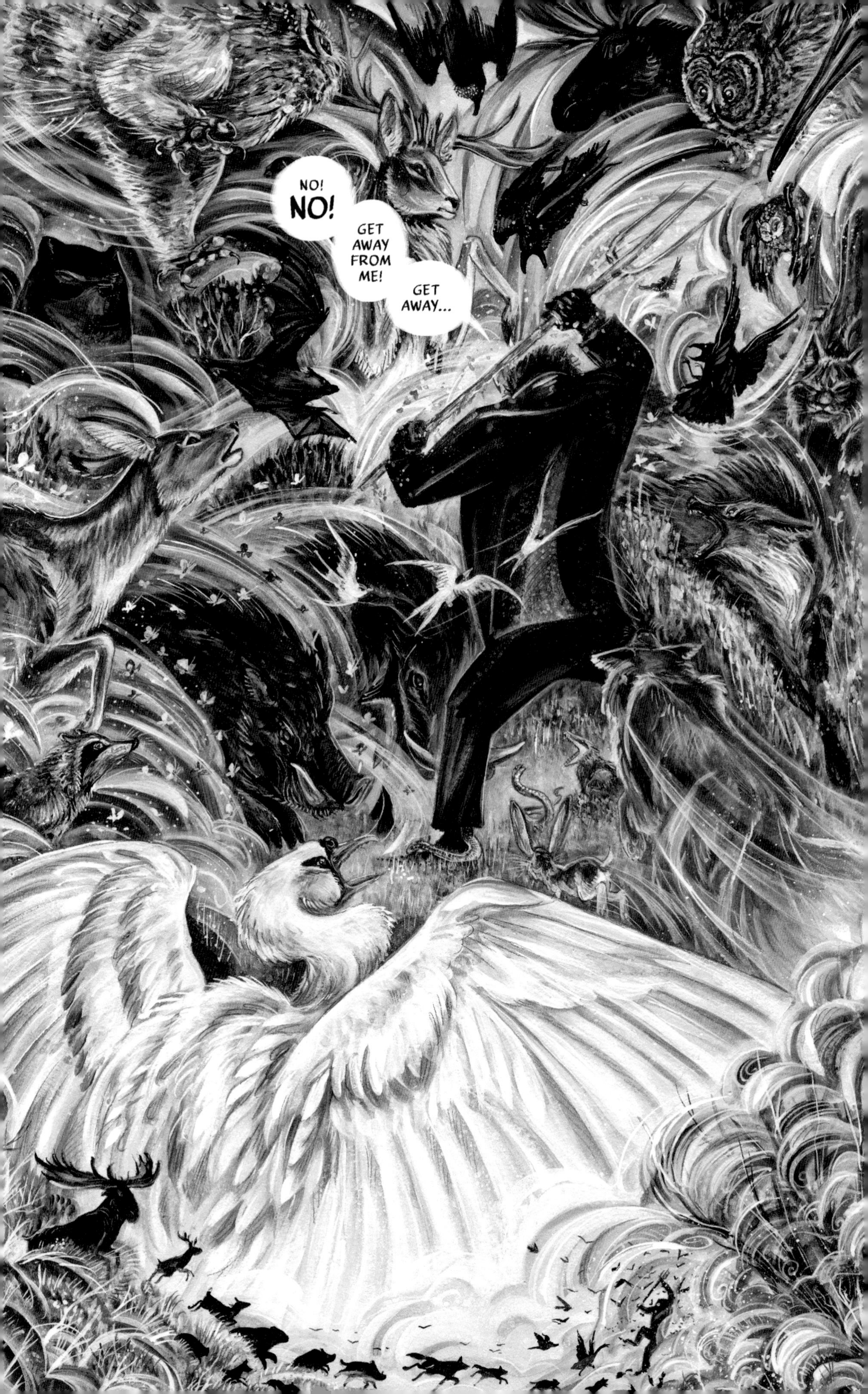
NO! NO!
GET AWAY FROM ME!
GET AWAY...

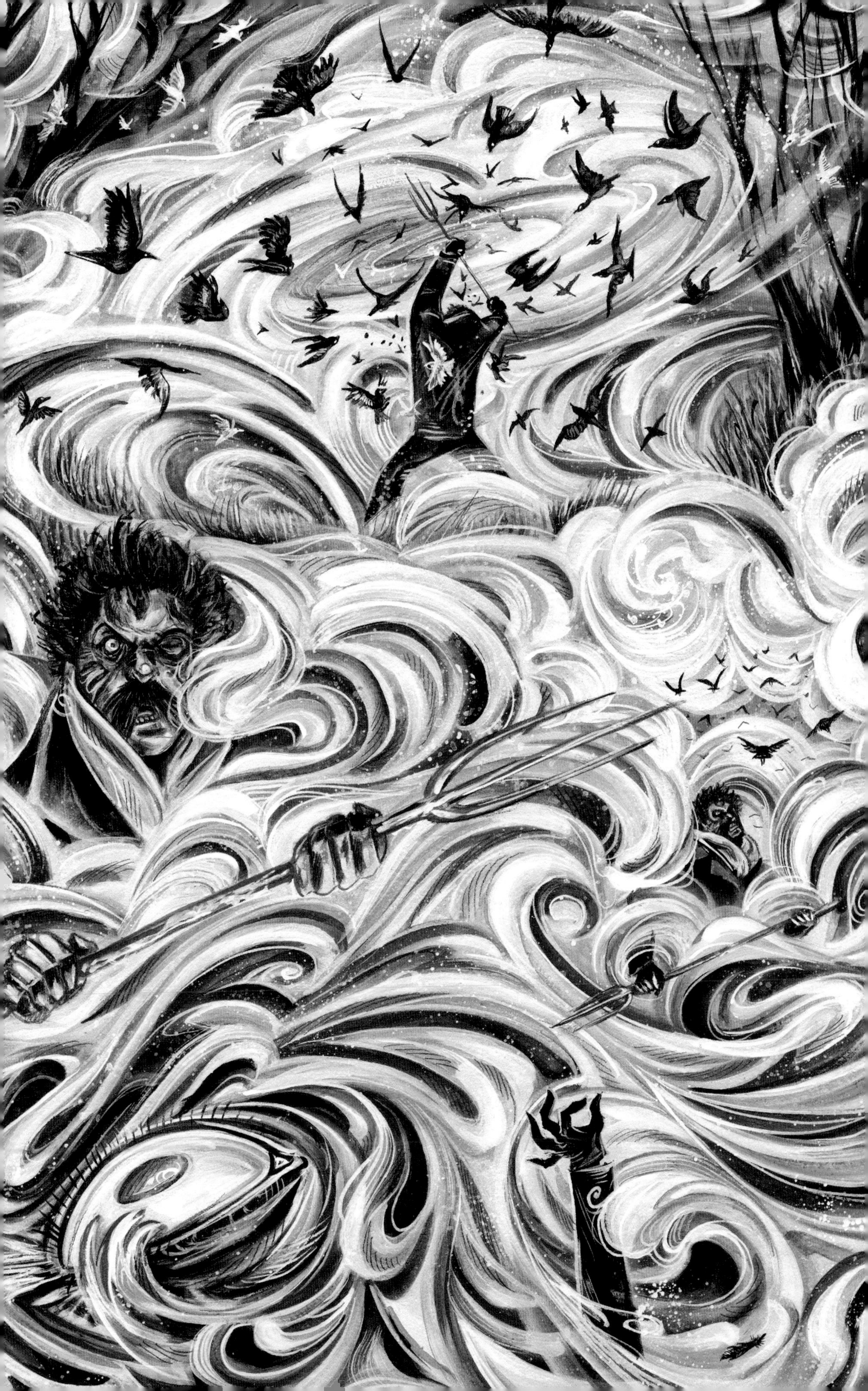

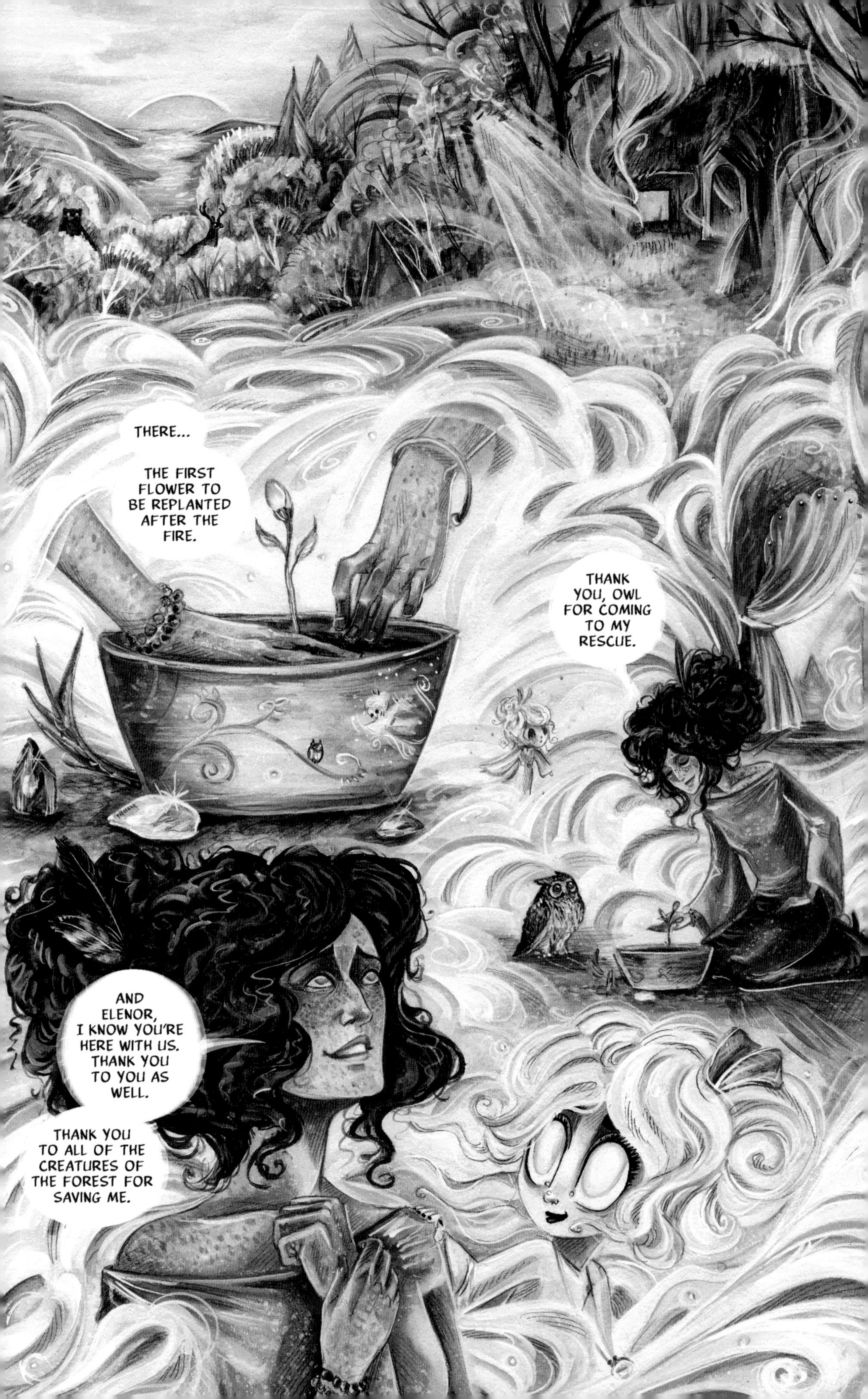

THERE...
THE FIRST FLOWER TO BE REPLANTED AFTER THE FIRE.
THANK YOU, OWL FOR COMING TO MY RESCUE.
AND ELENOR, I KNOW YOU'RE HERE WITH US. THANK YOU TO YOU AS WELL.
THANK YOU TO ALL OF THE CREATURES OF THE FOREST FOR SAVING ME.

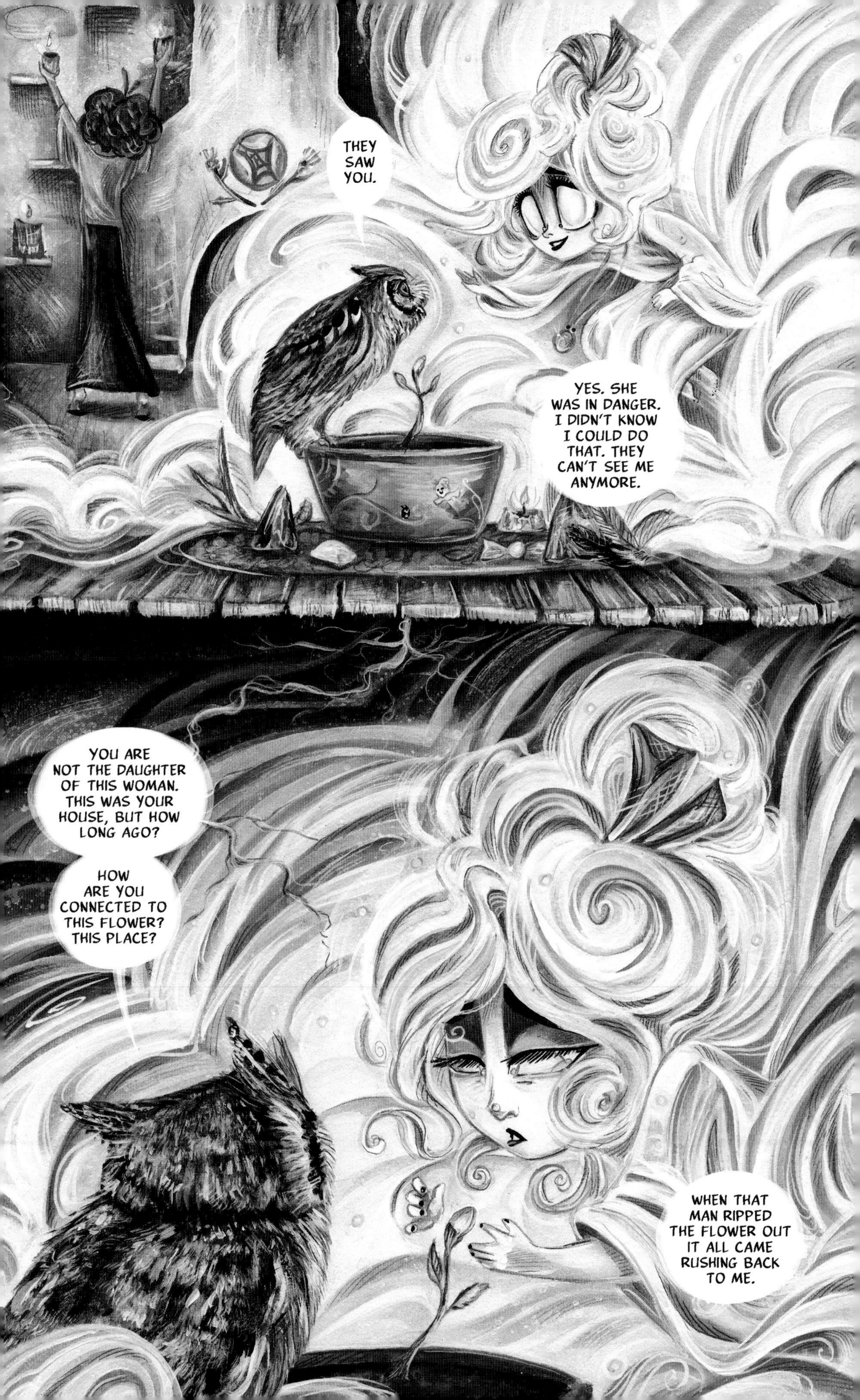
THEY SAW YOU.
YES. SHE WAS IN DANGER. I DIDN'T KNOW I COULD DO THAT. THEY CAN'T SEE ME ANYMORE.
YOU ARE NOT THE DAUGHTER OF THIS WOMAN. THIS WAS YOUR HOUSE, BUT HOW LONG AGO?
HOW ARE YOU CONNECTED TO THIS FLOWER? THIS PLACE?
WHEN THAT MAN RIPPED THE FLOWER OUT IT ALL CAME RUSHING BACK TO ME.

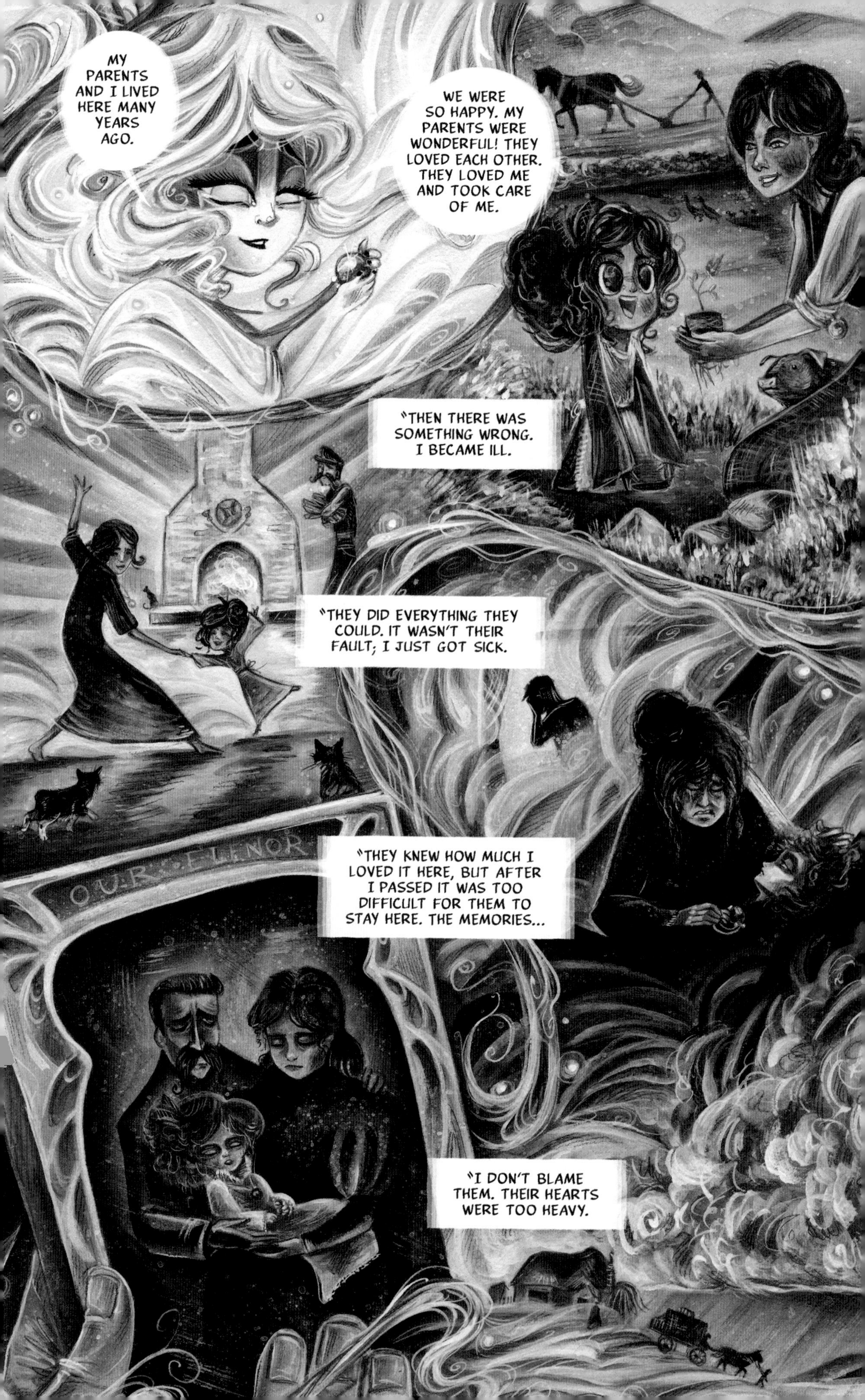
MY PARENTS AND I LIVED HERE MANY YEARS AGO.
WE WERE SO HAPPY. MY PARENTS WERE WONDERFUL! THEY LOVED EACH OTHER. THEY LOVED ME AND TOOK CARE OF ME.
"THEN THERE WAS SOMETHING WRONG. I BECAME ILL.
"THEY DID EVERYTHING THEY COULD. IT WASN'T THEIR FAULT; I JUST GOT SICK.
OUR ELINOR
"THEY KNEW HOW MUCH I LOVED IT HERE, BUT AFTER I PASSED IT WAS TOO DIFFICULT FOR THEM TO STAY HERE. THE MEMORIES...
"I DON'T BLAME THEM. THEIR HEARTS WERE TOO HEAVY.

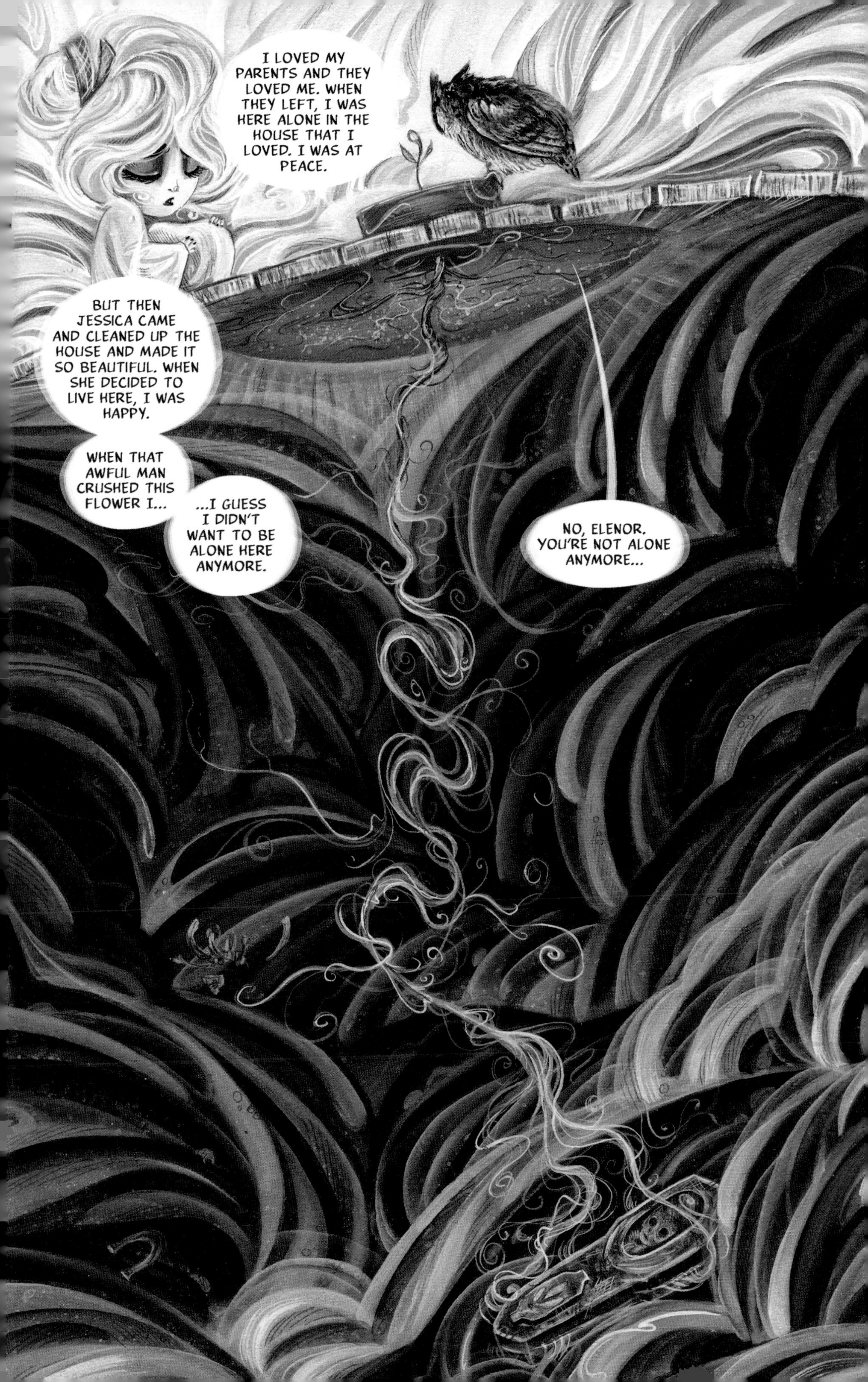

I LOVED MY PARENTS AND THEY LOVED ME. WHEN THEY LEFT, I WAS HERE ALONE IN THE HOUSE THAT I LOVED. I WAS AT PEACE.
BUT THEN JESSICA CAME AND CLEANED UP THE HOUSE AND MADE IT SO BEAUTIFUL. WHEN SHE DECIDED TO LIVE HERE, I WAS HAPPY.
WHEN THAT AWFUL MAN CRUSHED THIS FLOWER I...
...I GUESS I DIDN'T WANT TO BE ALONE HERE ANYMORE.
NO, ELENOR. YOU'RE NOT ALONE ANYMORE...

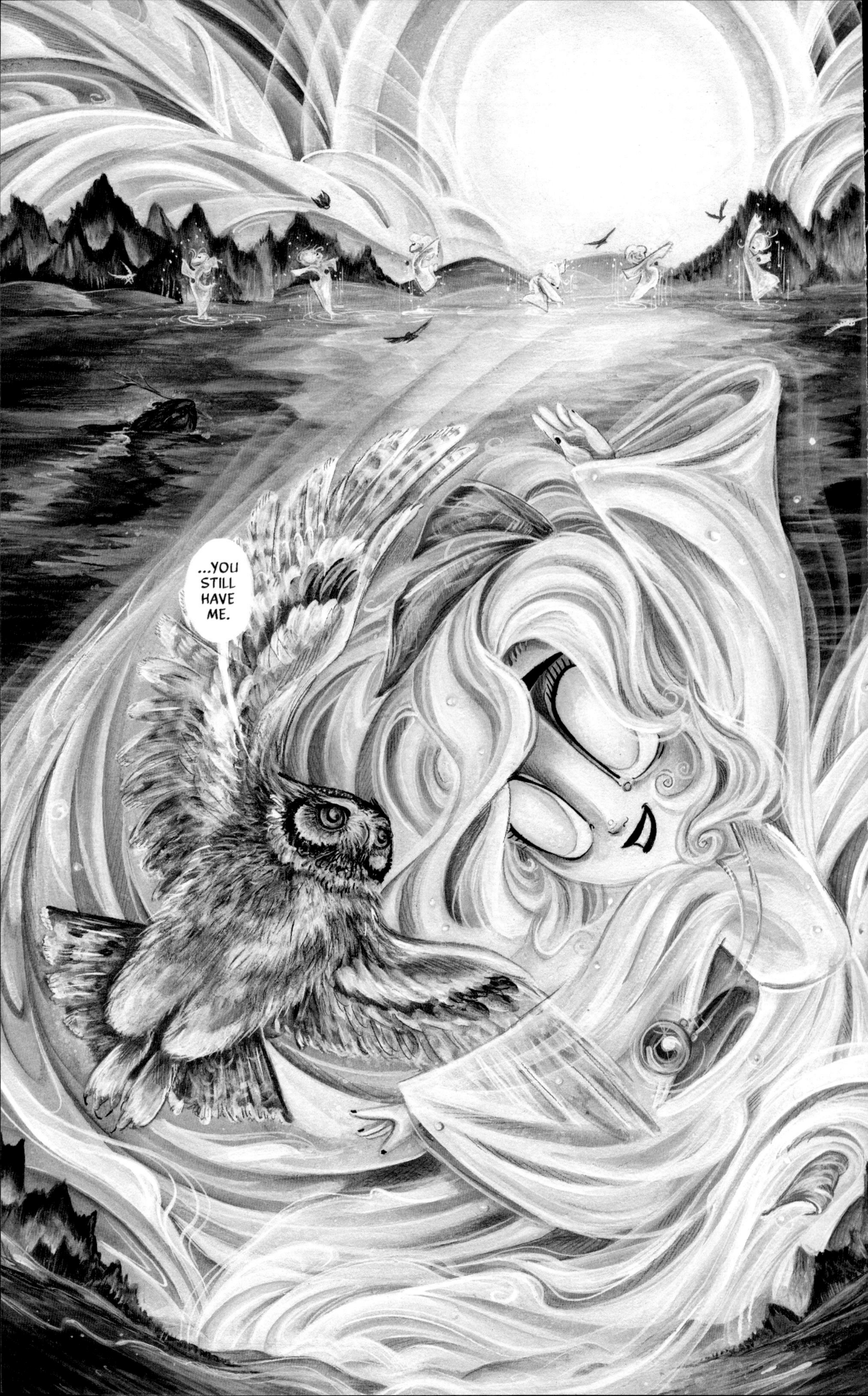
...YOU STILL HAVE ME.